Praise for the Red Carpet Catering Mystery Series

"The Red Carpet Catering series delivers a buffet of appealing characters, irresistible movie-industry details, and tantalizing plot twists. As delicious as a gourmet meal—and leaves you hungry for more!"

– Susan O'Brien,
Agatha Award-Nominated Author of *Finding Sky*

"Movie lovers, this is your book! Engaging and high-spirited, Penelope Sutherland never expected that catering for the cast and crew of a top-flight movie would lead to...murder. Great fun."

– Terrie Farley Moran,
Agatha Award-Winning Author of *Caught Read-Handed*

"With a nice island flavor, a nice puzzling mystery and a great cast of characters, this was a very enjoyable read."

– *Dru's Book Musings*

"A fast-paced cozy easily read and enjoyed in an afternoon...with Simmons' picturesque writing style you can almost taste the salt in the air. Take a vacation and join Penelope."

– *The Reading Room*

"Such a fun book. The characters are very likable and the writing is very well-done. Think of it as a cozy behind the scenes."

– *Booklikes*

"Delicious! A great read written by someone who knows the behind the scenes world of filmmaking...A winner!"

– Kathryn Leigh Scott,
Author of the Jinx Fogarty Mysteries

"This series is so well done that you will feel as though you have just gone to a friend's house to visit for a few hours."

— *The Reading Room*

"Loved this book! The characters are well-drawn and it's cleverly plotted. Totally engrossing...I felt as though I was actually on a movie set. The author is well-versed in her setting and she is able to keep the reader in suspense. I can't wait for the second book in the series."

— Marianna Heusler,
Edgar-Nominated Author of *No End to Trouble*

"Much of what makes this such an enjoyable new mystery is the background information on both catering and movie-making. Equally compelling is just how seamlessly author Simmons works Penelope into the investigation...this is a fun new series for readers who enjoy their theatrical showbiz mysteries with a culinary twist."

— *Kings River Life Magazine*

"A fun mystery on a movie set and delightful chef with delicious sounding food....Shawn Reilly Simmons has a flair!"

— Penn State Librarian

"With a likeable cast of characters and an inside look at the movie industry, this was equally entertaining and engaging."

— *Dru's Book Musings*

"Simmons has given us quite a good beginning to a new series; she manages to create characters that are both believable and likable while weaving in small tidbits of movie-making and what is involved in catering food to a movie crew...Highly recommended."

— *Any Good Book*

MURDER
ON THE
CHOPPING
BLOCK

The Red Carpet Catering Mystery Series
by Shawn Reilly Simmons

MURDER
ON THE
CHOPPING
BLOCK

A RED CARPET CATERING MYSTERY

SHAWN REILLY
SIMMONS

HENERY PRESS

For my sister, Erin

ACKNOWLEDGMENTS

As always I had a lot of help writing this book, beginning with my wonderful editor, Maria Edwards. I'm beyond grateful for her patient and kind guidance, and for showing me the way when I thought I'd written myself into a corner I couldn't get out of.

I'm extremely fortunate to have constant support from a wonderful group of crime writers that I'm lucky to call friends. They're there for a first read of a manuscript, or a word of encouragement on a particularly difficult day or week, or a discussion about a plot tangle over lunch or cocktails. I know they have my back, and they know who they are.

The best thing about being a mystery-crime writer is the wonderfully welcoming community you get to be a part of. In addition to writers, there are bloggers, reviewers, booksellers, readers, and fans I get to interact with at various events throughout the year. I can't thank them enough, particularly Dru Ann Love, Kristopher Zgorski, Kathy Harig, Cynthia Chow, Shana Gray, Kelly Letourneau, Pam Edmondson, Mary Louise Bishop, Deb Beamer, and Susan McAvoy Hannon.

Much love and thanks go out to Kendel Lynn and Art Molinares at Henery Press for continuing to believe in me and Penelope. I feel nurtured and appreciated, which fuels the creative fire.

My books always revolve around the theme of family, the one you're born with and the one you put together on your own. When we were just starting out in New York as young women, my sister and I cooked together in a lot of kitchens. We both have families of our own now, and close friends we've made along the way. I'm grateful to have had those experiences, and love the families we both have created, this far down the road.

Happy reading!

Shawn

CHAPTER 1

"If you push my lead actor off of that cliff, we're going to end up way over budget," Chad Hathaway shouted from behind his monitor. "I don't want to become Enemy Number One in Australia. Keep away from the edge, would you? Both of you, take a few steps in."

Penelope Sutherland looked up from her cutting board and watched the two actors, teetering near the edge of the rocky incline, pause, then fall back into their heated argument, the same one they'd read through at least a dozen times over the past couple of hours. They were ignoring the director's safety warnings again, like he hadn't spoken at all.

Penelope could recite the actors' lines herself word for word, because she'd already heard them so many times. The two of them had changed their delivery, but the words were always the same. This take, the man with the gun was shouting, spittle flying from his lips, and the one with his hands up in the air, pleading for his life, spoke quietly, reminding the other of all the good times they'd had together. With each take of the scene, they got closer to the steep incline, the Pacific Ocean churning two hundred feet below the cliff.

Chad sat slouched in his folding director's chair, hands on knees, his bony white knuckles stretching through his red freckled skin. A ring of sweat dampened the neck of his light grey t-shirt as he leaned forward at a sharp angle and stared at the screen. His resting facial expression was a pinched grimace, and when he was on set, it ranged from mildly irritated to hotly furious throughout the day, depending on how well, or not well, things were going. Even when they were on break, Chad seemed put out by everything and everyone around him.

"Cut!" Chad screamed, jumping up from his chair. His nervous energy radiated hotly from his wiry frame. "Reset the scene, twenty feet away from where you're standing. Right now."

Penelope looked back down at her board and ran her knife through the last cucumber, the blade moving like hot metal through butter, making a rapid tapping sound against the oil-rubbed wood creating a fan of perfectly uniform cucumber rounds.

"I'm touched you're so worried about me, Chaddie," Sebastian Beauregard, the star of the film, said, then broke into a laugh. He tapped his scene partner, Isaac Lee, on the shoulder and motioned him to move away from the edge. "Come on, mate. Let's not give old Chaddie boy a heart attack today. He looks like he's right on the edge himself."

Isaac, who was a shade taller than Sebastian, obliged by moving in a few paces. His well-tailored suit and crisp white shirt managed to look un-wilted despite the shimmering heat. The nickel-plated prop gun in his hand caught a ray of the sun and burned a slash across Penelope's eyes.

"Haven't we done this scene enough?" Isaac asked. "I'm still in vacation mode, mate."

"That's right. Where did you get off to again?" Sebastian teased. "Some tropical paradise with a saucy little Sheila, right? You've got that look about you. Like a man newly in love."

"Focus on your own affairs," Isaac said, his cheeks reddening. "You know I'm a gentleman, and gentlemen don't kiss and tell. You'd be wise to follow that advice."

"Would you two knock it off? We need the scene in the can," Chad said testily from his chair. He had a habit of speaking to the images of the actors on the screen, instead of the real-life versions in front of him.

"Come on," Isaac groaned. "I could use a coffee, get my first-day-back-to-work kinks ironed out."

"It would be great if I could get both of you to focus!" Chad yelled at the screen. Everyone in the director's tent froze, except for the cinematographer next to Chad, who dropped his head into his hands and raked his fingers through his sweaty hair.

"You're going to have to edit the hell out of this shot so it looks like we were standing in the same spot the whole time," Sebastian retorted. "The light is way off over here. Aren't you picking up all of these shadows on my face?"

Penelope glanced at Chad and watched his fairly freckled neck turn dark red.

"You just stick to getting the scene right," Chad said, sarcasm coating his words. He grabbed a clipboard the PA behind him was holding and tore through the first two pages. "Leave the actual directing of the film to me. The director."

Sebastian crossed his arms and chuckled, his suit jacket straining across his broad shoulders. After a minute of uneasy silence, he shook his head and brushed his hands down his lapels. "A director is supposed to capture the action of the talent, not stare at a screen all day."

The PA's mouth dropped open and he looked down at Chad, who tore off more pages from the clipboard and began crushing them in his fists. Penelope straightened up, her knife suspended over the cutting board, her gaze shifting from Chad to Sebastian and back again. Isaac took a few subtle steps away from Sebastian and looked out over the cliff, taking in the view of the ocean. A wave crashed against the rocks below them, which was the only sound heard during those thirty awkward seconds.

Penelope had watched Chad and Sebastian go at it more than once on this shoot, usually resulting in Sebastian storming off to his trailer, then sometimes not showing up on time the following day, or at all, depending on how bad the blowup was. The friction between the lead actor and director had already caused a number of production delays, and more reshoots than she'd ever remembered having to do. All of which cost the studio money. Chad was the third director they'd hired for this movie, and to his credit, the one who had stayed on the set the longest. Penelope quietly rooted for Chad, hoping he could get to the end of production without being fired or walking off the set like the other two directors before him.

Chad stood up from his chair and raised his palms in the air. "We all want the same thing here, Sebbie." He shrugged and snatched his headphones from the back of his chair, slipping them over his reedy neck. "We'll get it right if we can all work together."

Sebastian stared at Chad for a few beats, his stubbly chin twitching into a reluctant smile. "Fine by me, Chad my man. Let's get this work done. And don't call me Sebbie. See if you can remember that."

"And I prefer Chad," the director said, squaring his shoulders.

"You can call me Izzy. Any of you. I like it," Isaac said, still gazing at the ocean.

Sebastian's lip curled into a smile. "Is that what she called you on your vacation, mate? Izzy?"

Isaac laughed, and the tension was broken. With an uneasy truce in place, the cast and crew collectively sighed and got back to work. Penelope's shoulders eased down away from her ears and she grabbed a red bell pepper from the bin next to her board and began chopping it into thin slices.

Sebastian trotted over to the edge of the cliff and wheeled his arms wildly, pretending to almost fall off the edge.

"It's not even that far down. I'd survive that fall. Nothing like back home, right mate?" Sebastian said with a laugh.

"Right," Isaac said, ignoring Sebastian's antics.

Chad shook his head and tossed his headphones back onto his chair. The PA pointed to something on a tablet and mumbled to him.

"Can I get some water over here? It's got to be a hundred degrees already," Chad shouted at Penelope, then went back to studying the tablet the assistant held out for him.

"Water for the director, please," Penelope said to Javier who had just stepped down from the kitchen truck that was parked behind the catering tent. He was one of two new chefs she'd hired since arriving in California, and he'd proven to be a strong addition to the crew over the past couple of months. Javier nodded sharply and hurried to the drinks station, with Penelope watching him out of the corner of her eye as she finished up her salad bar prep.

"Army," he'd said in the interview when she asked where he learned to cater for large numbers of people.

"And can you tell me a little about that experience?" Penelope asked as she'd scanned through his CV.

"The weather was unpredictable, mostly hot, with the occasional sandstorm to deal with. There were one hundred and twenty-seven soldiers in my unit. I had to get meals ready quickly. We cooked at all hours, day and night, depending on the mission, and we had to pick up and move camp without a lot of warning," Javier had said.

"That sounds very similar to what we do," Penelope had said.

Javier had smiled and looked at the toes of his boots, his hands clasped at the small of his back. "I can handle anything you ask of me, ma'am."

Penelope had hired him on the spot. He had a quiet reserved manner, and was in no way aggressive, something she'd assumed he might be considering his military training. Javier had managed to prove her instincts right every day since, showing up for work earlier than he needed to and managing everything that was asked of him above and beyond her expectations.

Penelope had brought Francis, her trusted sous chef, out with her from their home base in New Jersey. He'd been with her since the beginning of Red Carpet Catering and she hadn't worked on a project without him yet.

Javier scooped up two water bottles from one of the iced-filled tubs under the table and brought them to Chad, the trail of water drips drying almost as soon as they hit the sandy ground. The sun was gaining strength, and more than one member of the crew had tied a damp towel around their neck to battle against the oppressive heat bearing down on them. Penelope tightened her long blonde ponytail and wiped a sheen of perspiration from her brow with the back of her forearm.

They'd been filming in and around Salacia Beach, California, a small community just north of Monterey featuring a rugged coastline and a string of mostly private beaches. Sebastian Beauregard was the next big thing out of Australia, or so Penelope had heard around the studio. Even though she'd worked in the film industry for several years, and was best friends with an A-list actress from an A-list acting family, she never quite understood how some actors hit it big while others fizzled out. How some worked steadily, seemingly without a break at all, while others worked every few years, or just faded away entirely. She had definitely not worked out how it could be predicted that someone she'd never heard of would very soon become a household name.

Sebastian appeared to be very well-known in his home country of Australia. He'd shown several of the crew articles and blog posts on his phone to support that fact. The movie they were filming now was just one of three high profile projects he'd been cast in, all set to release over the next two years. Penelope had to admit he was very handsome, in a roguish kind of way. He reminded her of a rebooted version of Cary Grant but less elegant. More like he could help you survive in the woods after a flood than use the right fork at dinner.

Things had improved on the set since Chad showed up, but Penelope would be happy when they got this one in the can and she could move on to a new project. They only had to get through two or three more weeks. Fingers crossed they could keep to schedule and wrap on time.

Javier stepped in front of Penelope's table and lifted his eyebrows as he tapped his wristwatch. She knew, without him saying a word, that he was concerned about lunch coming out late for the crew, even though the delay was not their fault.

Penelope shrugged and flicked her eyes toward Chad as she scraped cucumber seeds from her cutting board into her waste bowl. Javier shook his head and went to straighten the already perfectly arranged basket of linen-wrapped silverware next to the drinks table.

"Another day in paradise, huh Boss?" Francis said under his breath as he emerged from the kitchen truck. He had a serving pan full of grilled chicken breasts, sliced into strips.

"Paradise lost maybe," Penelope joked as she breathed in

the salty air. She finished arranging the salad toppings she'd prepared into bright white bowls. "It is beautiful out here, though, you have to admit."

Francis set the pan of chicken down on top of the warmer. "I guess. If you're into the whole fresh air, outdoors thing."

Penelope laughed. "You don't like being outside, city kid?"

"What?" Francis laughed. "I love it. But New Jersey air has more, I don't know...texture."

"Texture," Penelope repeated, suppressing a grin. "I guess that's one way to describe the oxygen back home." She wiped her hands on her apron and pulled her phone from her back pocket, checking the time. "Admit it, you're homesick," she said to Francis.

Francis sighed. "Yeah, I miss home," he said wistfully. "My girl's coming out this weekend, though. She wants to drive up to Napa, visit some wineries."

"That will be fun," Penelope suggested.

The sound of excited shouts pulled her attention back to the cliff. She sucked in a breath when she saw Sebastian wheeling his arms again, but this time the look on his face wasn't smug amusement, but surprised shock. Isaac lunged for him, grasping his lapels and pulling him forcefully, tumbling backwards, the both of them tripping over their feet.

"What are you doing, man? I told you to stay away," Chad yelled.

"And I told you it wasn't that dangerous," Sebastian said in an unnaturally loud voice. He swiped at his jacket lapels in a slapping motion, his hands shaking. Isaac stepped away from him, his hands on his hips, once again searching for something on the horizon.

"This movie is going to be the death of me," Chad said, shaking his head. He drank from his water bottle and stared at his leading man, who had almost fallen off a cliff, to prove some kind of point, Penelope assumed.

She watched Sebastian as he headed toward the mobile trailer parked at the edge of the rocky clearing, his strides long and his swagger, while still confident, a bit less sturdy than usual.

Penelope saw a flash of terror on Sebastian's face in the split second after he was pulled back from the edge, realizing too late he probably wouldn't survive a fall like that after all.

CHAPTER 2

Penelope stared at the bumper sticker on the car in front of her as she waited for the red light to turn. It was of two happy faces with scrawled type in the center that read *Have a Nice Day*. But the word "Nice" had a line through it, which she supposed was meant to tell her to just have a day. Although the day she'd just had hadn't been particularly nice, it was over, and she was happy to be headed back to her temporary home in Salacia Beach on California's rugged central coast. The light changed and a few turns later she was on her street, Chardonnay Court, a cul-de-sac shaped like a flat circle. The sight of her well-maintained beach house lifted her spirits as she slowed to approach the short driveway. There were only two houses on the court, a modern, tower-like home made of blue-tinted glass overlooking the ocean, and a much smaller beach bungalow a few hundred yards to the right of it where Penelope was staying.

As she pulled into the driveway, the woman's voice on the radio said, "Today on *Unsolved California*, we're crowdsourcing with you all for clues to two murders that happened just over fifteen years ago."

"Oh, the double homicide in La Brea?" her co-host replied. "Yeah, that's a good one."

The two women on the radio debated what made the La Brea murders unique and outlined the details of the crime. Penelope idled in the driveway and pulled the cord from her radio, unplugging her phone, then pressed the button for the garage door. She'd listen to the rest of the episode on the way into work in the morning. She'd gotten hooked on the true crime podcast during her commutes back and forth to Salacia Beach and the surrounding locations where they had filmed, and to the production studio, a large space converted warehouse that had previously housed a fish canning factory. The podcasters talked about a different unsolved murder each week with a case that had gone cold, and asked their listeners to logon to their website or call in to offer theories and suggestions, or even actual clues.

Something caught her eye and she turned her head toward the large house down the street. The front door was open, something she hadn't noticed when she pulled into their street. As the garage door rumbled up on its track, a shadow moved behind the neighbor's front window. The couple next door had both been away the past two weeks, but must have returned.

Penelope eased inside the garage and pressed the button again, watching it close all the way from inside the BMW. She'd left her trusty Jeep back in her home garage in New Jersey after the production company had included the use of a rental car in her contract. Francis had driven the kitchen truck out to California. Penelope had told him to take his time on the way out, stop and do some sightseeing and rest as much as he wanted. He'd done the drive in three days, anxious to get set up in his temporary apartment on the beach. That had been back in the spring, and now they were almost finished, their time on the West Coast coming to a close.

The buzz surrounding Sebastian and *Severed Lives* had gotten buzzier over the past couple of weeks. Someone on the set had leaked a couple of stories detailing Sebastian's behavior, and the perceived trouble on the set. Which only set Chad further on edge. Even though she loved living in this beautiful place in this cute little house, Penelope thought she'd be relieved to pack up and head back east when all was said and done.

Grabbing a canvas grocery bag from the back seat, Penelope clicked the fob, and kept her keys in her hand, the silver spoke of one wedged between her second and third fingers. She tested the doorknob and it tensed under her hand. Penelope knew she'd pulled the door closed and made sure it had locked before she'd left for work twelve hours earlier, but it was always good to be cautious, especially for a woman living alone, three thousand miles from home. Setting the bag on the kitchen counter, she turned to the refrigerator and pulled out a bottle of sparkling water, taking a long sip before sighing and setting it down on the sandstone island countertop.

After putting the groceries away, Penelope stepped out onto her back patio and gazed at her pool, enjoying the relative quiet surrounding her home and shaking off the tension of the workday. The ocean boomed against the rocks below her house, and she breathed in the salt-tinged air.

When Chad called cut and wrapped for the day, he announced they'd be right back there tomorrow, reshooting the entire fight scene between Sebastian and Isaac. Chad was unhappy with the dailies he viewed, so the filming day had essentially been wasted. Chad explained after a few groans from the crew that it was the most important scene in the movie, and it had to be right, or they'd have a flop on their hands.

Severed Lives was supposed to go into wide release the following summer, if the producers were still behind it when they saw the final cut. It was a thriller about an FBI agent, played by Sebastian, who'd gone rogue and was trying to solve a string of murders up and down the California coast. Isaac was playing Sebastian's brother, who was the prime suspect in the killings. Sebastian played the part of rogue very well, Penelope thought as she took another sip of water.

She had been given a copy of the script on the first day of filming, and had read it propped up in bed the first night after work, unable to put it down.

Penelope sat down on the slate tile surrounding the pool and dipped her feet into the water, warm as a bath, and pulled out her phone. She hadn't talked to her boyfriend all day, and had the sudden urge to talk to him for hours, to listen to his familiar comforting voice until she fell asleep that night.

"Leave a message and I'll call you back," Joey's voice buzzed in her ear.

"Straight to voicemail?" she mumbled, staring at the screen. She typed a text letting him know she was home for the day and to call her back, then set down the phone on the patio and went inside to put on her bathing suit.

CHAPTER 3

Penelope's arms slid beneath the surface of the water as she pulled herself forward through the lap. She turned her head to the side and exhaled, then ducked her face again as she approached the edge of the saltwater pool for the tenth time. She'd gotten into the habit of swimming laps before dinner, enjoying how the water relaxed and cooled her down after the long hot days cooking on the film set. She caught herself thinking about swimming laps during work.

As she neared the edge of the pool, she coasted to the wall, touching the slate with her water-pruned fingers. Swiping the slightly salty water from her eyes with one hand, she felt something on the other that caused her to jerk it up from the slate tiles.

Wiping a few more drops of water from her face she took a deep breath to calm her rapid heartbeat. Right next to her evaporating handprint was a long-haired black cat with dark green eyes that languidly stared up at her.

"What are you doing here, little one?" Penelope said, pressing her hand to her chest. The sun had begun to set over the ocean and the air was cool against her wet skin. "You gave me a fright."

The cat blinked once and purred in response. The cat had on a bright pink leather collar with a platinum nametag dangling from it, the name Mirabella etched in the center with a small diamond dotting the "i." Penelope wondered if the diamond was real. Glancing at the three-story glass beach house next door, she decided it probably was. Penelope walked up the steps out of the pool and grabbed a towel. Mirabella stretched out on the tiles and curved her body into an inverted "C," showing Penelope her belly. Penelope reached down and rubbed it, then stood up and stretched her arms over her head.

Mirabella sprung up from the ground and tapped her paw on Penelope's bare foot.

"You're such a sweetie, aren't you?" Penelope said, reaching down to give her a rub behind the ears.

Mirabella leaned into Penelope's hand and rubbed her head against it.

"Mirabella!" A man's voice shouted from the other side of the wall separating Penelope's patio from the one next door.

The cat ignored the voice and purred louder, pressing harder into Penelope's hand.

"He's looking for you again, you little runaway," Penelope said. Her hair dripped onto the patio as she wrapped herself in the towel. "Calvin?" Penelope called toward the wall. It was adobe, the same color as her house, and was too tall for Penelope to see over. "Mirabella is over here again."

"I'm sorry, Penelope. I don't know why she thinks she has the run of your place too," Calvin said. "She's a little Houdini, this one."

"It's no problem. I like getting visits from her. I was just finishing my swim," Penelope said. "You can come on through if you like." She tucked her towel firmly under her arms and headed toward the side gate next to the house. Penelope could hear his footsteps crunching on the fine gravel that lined both sides of the fence.

"Come on, sweetie," Penelope said in a soft voice. Mirabella stared at her, acting like she wasn't going to follow, then rose up on stiff legs and strutted toward the gate as if it was her idea in the first place.

Penelope unhooked the latch and pulled open the gate. Her neighbor, and employer on the movie, Calvin Pope, stood on the other side. He was shirtless, his chest tan beneath a nest of white hair, and was wearing a pair of green swimming trunks. An infinity pool glowed bright blue behind him, the surface looking like polished glass. Penelope glanced at the view beyond the edge of the pool where the sun was continuing its descent into the ocean. Streaks of bright orange and purple colored the sky.

Calvin smiled widely. There was a purplish tinge to his teeth, and a half-full glass of wine in his hand.

"Welcome home, Calvin," Penelope said. "Did you have a good trip?"

"I did, thanks," Calvin said. "Not a bad flight back at all. It's always good to be home, though. New York is so dirty. Brogan is less thrilled to be back from her little jaunt overseas. She still thinks of New Zealand as her home, even though we've been living here for years now."

Penelope made a sympathetic sound. "I suppose she is really far away from her family," she said. Penelope herself didn't have a large or particularly close family, but she thought that if she did, she'd prefer to be less than a fourteen-hour flight away.

"I like living on this side of the world myself," Calvin continued, as if he hadn't heard her. "No matter how much my wife would like us to move back."

Penelope looked away, in the hopes that the conversation would end there. Mirabella made a figure eight around Penelope's damp ankles.

"This cat...she's devious," he said with a sigh. "Running off is her way of rebelling when she thinks she's been hemmed in too long, no matter how good she has it at home. She's angry with us for leaving, and even angrier when we return."

Penelope smiled. "She's very sweet. I'm sure she's glad to see you both home."

Calvin took a sip of his wine then clucked a scolding tongue at his cat. Mirabella stopped her circling and sat primly on the patio next to Penelope's feet and looked up at him.

"Okay, we're off." He scooped her up and kissed the fuzz on top of her head, then hoisted her onto his broad shoulders. She nuzzled his ear then curled behind his neck, her tail flicking against his chest. Calvin was rugged and muscular, his blond hair just beginning to turn silver. In his younger years Calvin had acted in over a dozen movies, and was now one of Hollywood's most sought after producers.

"Why don't you come over?" Calvin said suddenly as he stroked Mirabella's tail. "Jacque brought dinner in this morning, some kind of chicken something or other. We're just meant to put it in the oven. Knowing our chef and his portion sizes, we'll never be able to eat it all. My daughter, Scarlett, might stop by, but you can't count on her to eat much."

"Well," Penelope said, picturing the Popes' chef, a tall slender Frenchman who came and stocked their fridge with meals a few days a week when the Popes were in town. He always made Penelope think of the old adage to never trust a skinny chef. "I don't want to impose on your family."

"Pshaw," Calvin said with a wave of his hand. "We love your company. And also I'd like to hear firsthand how things have been going on the set."

"Okay," Penelope said, hesitantly. She'd just decompressed from the day and was hoping to stay that way for at least the evening. "You're sure you're not too worn out from your trip?"

"Not at all. I've only been in New York for development meetings, a few set visits. It's Brogan who'll be dealing with the jetlag. And for some reason, it doesn't affect her hardly at all. Must be all the kale she eats or all the sparkling water at eight dollars a bottle," he said, accompanied by an eye roll.

"Maybe you should check with Brogan first," Penelope suggested.

"No. It's decided. Let us, well, let Jacque cook for you. You can tell us if we're paying too much for his services."

Penelope laughed then pressed her fingers to her lips. "Okay, sounds good. I just have to get changed."

"I've just opened a bottle of Rothschild, and Brogan doesn't want any. It won't be as good tomorrow, once the air gets to it. Help me drink some of my welcome home wine."

"Welcome home wine?" Penelope asked, eyeing his glass. She'd seen bottles with that particular label reach into the thousands of dollars. Calvin must really like treating himself if he opened wines like that on a regular basis.

"I open a bottle of this whenever I get home," Calvin said, "to remind myself to be grateful for what I have."

"That's a nice tradition," Penelope said. "I'll be right over."

"Brilliant!" Calvin said loudly. Mirabella blinked at Penelope and purred. "See you shortly." He turned abruptly and headed for the gate, whistling as he stepped back through to his own backyard.

CHAPTER 4

"Calvin said you were coming for dinner," Brogan Pope said as she swung open the front door. She pulled Penelope into a tight hug then tugged her over the threshold. Calvin's wife was short with deeply tanned skin and shiny black hair that stood out around her head in untamable curls. Penelope wasn't tall, but felt like she towered over her petite neighbor.

The scent of chicken braising in wine wafted down the hallway toward them.

"*Coq au vin*?" Penelope guessed. After a quick shower, she'd changed into a simple jade-colored cotton sundress and tied her damp hair into a loose bun on top of her head.

"Got it in one, Chef," Brogan said. "Come on through. Calvin is back there somewhere." She led Penelope through the foyer toward the kitchen, the long flowing skirt of her wrap dress skimming the shiny wood floor. Penelope slid out of her sandals and left them by the front door, then followed the barefoot Brogan down the hallway.

In the great room at the back of the house overlooking the ocean was a spiral stairway leading to the second and third levels. It was made of blue-tinted glass, so a person on the stairs looked like they were floating on air. On a previous visit to her neighbors' house, Brogan had shown Penelope a featured spread of the house that had been showcased in an interior design magazine. Even though she didn't know much about architecture, Penelope could tell the Popes' property was unique.

"How was New Zealand?" Penelope asked after taking a seat at the dining room table. Everything in the kitchen gleamed white with blue accents, the same shade as the stairs. The tropical colors of Brogan's outfit vibrated against the muted background of her kitchen.

Brogan placed her hands on the soapstone counter. "Fine. Good." There were faint circles under her big brown eyes, but otherwise Brogan looked vibrant and healthy, not like she'd just flown over the ocean for most of a day. She'd tried to tame her hair by tying it with a scarf, but strands had already pulled loose, in defiance of her efforts. A silver necklace with a bird charm, its wings spread wide in flight, glittered against her dark skin.

Calvin appeared from behind the fireplace and went into the kitchen, slipping his arms around Brogan's thin waist. She laughed and tried to wriggle away from him, but Calvin held her in place and kissed her on the cheek. "How I missed you, my love."

"Go on, pay attention to the guest you invited to dinner," Brogan said, pushing him away again. He released her and shook his head, then slid open a drawer on the island and took out a wine opener. Penelope guessed Brogan was more than twenty years younger than Calvin, maybe more, but she forgot about their age difference when she saw them together. They always seemed at ease around each other.

"Thanks for feeding me tonight," Penelope said. "I hadn't thought about dinner yet."

"Of course," Brogan said. "It was my idea to invite you."

Penelope accepted a glass of wine from Calvin and took a

seat at the long white kitchen table that backed up to one of the soaring windows.

"No, it was my idea," Calvin mumbled under his breath. Then he said louder, "It couldn't possibly have been your idea, my love, because I only thought of it when I was at Penelope's house just now, retrieving your misbehaving cat. The one who is constantly bothering the neighbors."

Brogan rolled her eyes again. "If you believe everything Calvin tells you, you'll own the Brooklyn Bridge or end up bobbing about on a fishing boat somewhere out in the middle of the Pacific."

"I've heard the bridge reference before, but a fishing boat? That's a new one," Penelope said after sipping her wine.

Calvin poured himself a tad more and set his glass down on the table next to her. He'd put on a t-shirt, but still wore his swim trunks.

"A fishing boat," Brogan said with a smirk. "When Calvin was a boy, he wanted to be a fisherman. Didn't you, Cal?"

"Now, now, my dear," Calvin said, waving his finger. "Don't go telling tales on me."

"Why not?" Brogan said, crossing her arms. "What's the point of being married to someone if you can't tease them from time to time? Anyway, like I was saying, Calvin tried to sweep me off my feet with tales of a life together on the ocean, when I already knew he was a suit in a big studio back home. I think he thought it made him sound rugged, and I'd find him more attractive."

"Yes, she'd had enough of the rugged life by the time I came around," Calvin said, raising his voice playfully. "But my love of the sea is how *Thriller Island* was conceived and born. So I was onto something."

"True enough," Brogan said with a nod before pulling open

the oven door. The smells of rendered bacon, mushrooms, and sautéed onions bathed in white wine made Penelope's mouth water.

"*Thriller Island.* I love that show," she said to fill the lull in conversation.

Calvin ducked his head and gave her a smile. "Thank you." He winked at the back of Brogan's head and Penelope laughed. "It's Scarlett's baby now. I've just passed my first-born show down to my first-born child."

"I didn't know Scarlett was interested in producing," Penelope said.

"She's just getting started," Calvin said. "Learning the ins and outs of production and management. She's my child, so of course she'd like to take over the reins today."

"She sure would," Brogan said under her breath, but loud enough for Penelope to hear.

"And she will, as soon as I leave this earthly plane or she makes enough to buy me out of the business, whichever comes first," Calvin said with a laugh. "Although the amount of money it would take to buy my shares is...well, let's just say it's not pocket change."

"Millions," Brogan whispered dramatically.

"My wife has no interest in running a production studio, do you dear?" Calvin said, a sharpness coming into his voice.

"I wouldn't know where to begin," Brogan said. "My talent lies in front of the camera not behind it. I have a feeling Scarlett could manage it, though. She's that special kind of driven, just like her father."

"Ah, speak of the devil..." Calvin said when the front door opened and a warm breeze stirred through the room. "The prodigal daughter returns."

"We're in the kitchen, Scarlett," Calvin called.

Calvin's daughter appeared in the hallway. She was dressed in a dark blue pant suit and low heels with an expensive looking briefcase dangling from a strap over her shoulder.

"Hi, Calvin," she said with a quick peck on his cheek. "Brogan."

"She hates calling me Dad for some reason," Calvin said behind his hand to Penelope.

"Glad you could make it," Brogan said from behind the counter, glancing down at Scarlett's shoes on the scuff-less wooden floor.

"Nice to see you again, Penelope," Scarlett said, reaching out her hand. Penelope stood up from her chair and extended her arm across the table. Scarlett's grip was hard, the skin on her hand chilled despite the warm air.

"We were just talking about *Thriller Island*," Calvin said, offering Scarlett a wine glass, which she waved away. Calvin set the glass on the table in front of her anyway.

"My best friend Arlena and I watch it whenever it's on," Penelope said. "It's amazing to see people surviving like that, out in the elements, having to fish and hunt. I don't think I could manage it."

"Yes," Scarlett said. "Some people can't manage in much less strenuous circumstances. With generous expense accounts even." She glanced at Brogan standing at the kitchen island. Brogan ignored her and studied her fingernails.

"To be fair, there are a few more things available to eat on the island than we let on to the viewers," Scarlett said with a tight smile. "We can't actually starve the contestants, but we can make them uncomfortable. Uncomfortable contestants make for good television."

"They don't have rules about when and what they can eat? I know for film it's very strict," Penelope said.

"The contestants on reality shows aren't in the actors' union or considered talent, so there's more leeway with how we can treat them," Brogan said with a satisfied nod.

"And some are more talented than others, of course." Calvin laughed loudly, and Brogan threw a barbed look at the father-daughter duo at her table. Brogan and Scarlett looked to be about the same age, and Penelope thought it was possible that Brogan might even be younger than her stepdaughter.

"Speaking of food, dinner's about ready," Brogan said, running a finger down a printed instruction sheet on the counter. "Are you staying for dinner, Scarlett?"

"No thanks," Scarlett said with some amusement. "I just wanted to go over that proposal with Calvin."

"Well, we're getting ready to eat very soon," Brogan said. "Jacque is so precise with the cooking instructions. One minute more and dinner will be ruined."

"It smells wonderful," Penelope offered. "Can I help with anything?"

"Brogan can manage," Calvin said, motioning for Scarlett to take a seat at the table. "You worked all day. Brogan spent the day in First Class drinking champagne cocktails. Right, love?" Scarlett poured herself a glass of water from a pitcher on the counter and sat down at the table.

Penelope watched Brogan's shoulders tense slightly before she folded the instructions and pulled open the oven again. Slipping on a pair of padded mitts, she pulled a large enameled cast iron pot from inside and set it on the island.

Penelope jumped up and grabbed a trivet from a drawer near the stove, then motioned for Brogan to pick it up again, sliding it beneath the scorching pan.

"Don't want to scorch your beautiful countertop," Penelope said.

Scarlett let out a huff. "Mustn't burn the house down, Brogan."

"Thanks," Brogan said tightly. "Maybe I am beginning to feel some jetlag after all."

Penelope wiped the edge of the counter with one of the towels and gazed at the casserole dish, not wanting to take any side in the tense family standoff.

"Excuse me a moment, won't you?" Brogan said. She floated over to the staircase and trotted up, her long skirt brushing the steps behind her.

"So," Calvin said, after watching his wife scurry upstairs and disappear into the master suite. "How have things been going on the set, Penelope?"

She studied Calvin's face, and the brush of silvery stubble that had just begun to show on his jawline. His skin was smooth and tan, his cheekbones high and his jaw strong, with no signs of softening like so many other men his age. Scarlett didn't look like him much at all, her features small and close. If Penelope didn't know any better, she'd say she looked more like her stepmother.

"It's been...an experience," Penelope began as she retook her seat at the table. "Nothing too bad has happened, but it feels more tense than other sets I've been on."

Calvin's expression became annoyed. "I think we made a mistake bringing on this Chad character. He was supposed to get everything wrapped up quickly but now it feels like he's slowed it down even more. Maybe I should fire him, too." Calvin eyed the staircase where Mirabella was descending, meowing loudly at the humans gathered on the first floor.

"Oh I didn't mean—" Penelope began.

"Sebastian can be a handful," Calvin said, his expression softening. "But he's the next Golden Goose, as they say, right now. He better be to justify the salary we're paying him. And Scarlett, honey, go easier on Brogan, would you? In front of company, especially."

Scarlett sniffed and took a sip her water. "What you see in her I've no—"

"Stop," Calvin said, and Scarlett did, her cheeks reddening slightly under the generous layer of foundation covering her pale skin.

"Well," Penelope said, hoping to begin a conversation that would cut the tension, "have you ever worked with Sebastian before?"

Calvin shook his head quickly. "No. I don't know him well, not personally anyway, only by reputation. But he's well known in Australia and New Zealand. Brogan had a bit part on a soap opera many years back that he starred in, when he was just another working actor on his way up."

"Here's hoping your bet pays off," Scarlett said, swirling the water in her glass like it was wine.

"You'll have made a good one if he's going to be a big star," Penelope said.

"You know, I haven't produced a ton of movies. I only take on the ones I really feel something about," Calvin said, eyes on his daughter. He pulled an unopened wine bottle toward him, dragging the bottom of it across the table.

"Speaking of things we feel something about," Scarlett said. "Can we talk about the show now? It's going to be a winner for Pope Productions."

Calvin nodded absently and studied the wine label. Penelope glanced at the last one he'd poured from and was surprised to see it nearly empty. Mirabella sat next to Penelope and gazed up at her from the floor.

"She eats after we do," Calvin said, eyeing the cat. "One of

Mother's rules."

"Brogan is strict with her?" Penelope said. "I don't think I could resist that cute face." She reached down and rubbed Mirabella's ears.

"You have no idea," Calvin muttered. "Thank goodness we have no human children of our own. They'd hate us."

Penelope kept her eyes on the cat, and hoped Brogan hadn't overheard that last comment from upstairs.

"We hope, Penelope," Scarlett said, "that this proposal I'm talking about will be of interest to you. When Calvin mentioned you'd be over for dinner I decided to swing by on my way home from the studio so we could chat about it."

Penelope sat up straighter, trying to think what this mysterious proposal could be. She knew her piece of the production had been going well, apart from the few times Sebastian wasn't happy with the day's meal selection and they had to make him a different meal off the main menu. But that wasn't unusual. She'd handled dozens of special requests on film sets. She leaned forward.

"We're putting a new culinary competition show into production," Scarlett said.

"Oh I love watching those," Penelope said.

Scarlett nodded. "The new take on ours will be a battle of elite chefs. Like a culinary dream team, from high end restaurants. They'll battle it out with each other, the grand prize being a head chef position at a new establishment we'll be creating, and fifty thousand dollars."

"That's exciting," Penelope said, intrigued.

"Would you consider taking a look at the show with us? We'd like you to consult on the concept, and give feedback on the contestants," Calvin said.

"Really?" Penelope asked.

"We think your input would be very valuable. None of us are chefs, or can even cook. But we do know how to produce reality shows that people watch," Scarlett said.

"My daughter is convinced we've got the winning formula for the next great cooking competition show, but the opinion of a culinary expert with your résumé would go a long way convincing our sponsors."

Penelope took a sip of her wine and considered what she'd just heard. "I've never done anything like that before. I'm not sure—"

"You're ideal," Calvin said. "You're an experienced chef with some very high-profile clients, and you're a trusted member of Pope Productions already. We value your opinion."

Penelope laughed. "Okay, I'd love to. If you're sure I could be of help."

"Absolutely," Calvin said, picking up the wine opener. "Right then. You're on the team."

Scarlett looked elated when Penelope had said yes. "You'll be on the executive team for the project. You'll get compensated as such, and you'll get a listing in the credits. If the project goes forward, of course."

"Credits?" Penelope asked.

"Of course, dear," Calvin said, twisting the wine opener in a circular motion. "Culinary consultant, something under the production category."

"Wow," Penelope said. "Thanks."

"No thanks necessary. You'll be helping us tremendously." Calvin opened the bottle and poured himself another splash of wine. He tapped his wine glass to hers and said, "You're an excellent chef, and you're good company as well."

"What are you scheming about down there?" Brogan called from the top of the stairs. She'd smoothed her hair back from her face, which looked a little drawn in the diminishing light.

"Just a plan to take over the world, darling," Calvin said. "You know, the usual."

Scarlett stood up from the table. "I'm off. Enjoy your dinner. Penelope, I'll touch base with you at the studio sometime next week."

"Great," Penelope said.

"That's enough work talk then," Brogan said as she stepped carefully down the stairs.

Scarlett left with a slight nod of the head toward Brogan.

"Now that things have quieted down, we can eat," Brogan said after they'd heard the front door close.

CHAPTER 5

Calvin watched her from his front door as Penelope walked the short distance back to her own house. It was technically on the property of the glass castle the Popes lived in, and had once served as a residence for the help of the original owners.

She'd thanked Calvin and Brogan for a lovely evening before heading out, her belly full from the delicious *coq au van* and her head buzzing pleasantly from the excellent wine and new job opportunity. Calvin had insisted on opening that second bottle, and every time Penelope's glass was almost empty, he'd top it off.

Penelope had always operated on gut instinct, all the way back to when she became personal chef to Arlena Madison several years before. It had been one of the best decisions she had ever made, had in fact brought her to the very spot she was standing in now. The Madison family had opened many doors for her as a chef, while also providing the large loving family that she'd always longed for.

When she got to her porch, she stopped short, and her heart leapt into her throat. Someone was there in the dark, the silhouette of a man rocking back and forth on the front porch chair.

"What are you doing here?" she stuttered, her words tumbling out before she could think.

Joey slid off the rocking chair. "Surprise," he said, a smile behind his words.

Penelope hurried up the steps and flung her arms around him, squeezing him to her.

"But...what are you doing here?" she repeated. "You weren't supposed to get in until Saturday."

Penelope stepped back and looked at him again, then pulled him in for another hug.

Joey laughed and swayed with her gently, the wooden porch creaking beneath their feet. "I couldn't wait to see you. We closed that big case and I took a few extra days off. Are you surprised?" Joey was a homicide detective back in New Jersey, but Penelope had known him since they were kids together in school. They'd reconnected a couple of years earlier, when a young girl had been left for dead in front of Penelope and Arlena's house. They'd been together ever since.

"Everything okay over there?" Calvin called from his porch. "You're not being attacked, are you, Penelope?"

She let go of Joey and spun around, a bubble of laughter rising in her chest.

"I'm fine, it's Joey, my boyfriend from back home," Penelope called.

"Nice to see you again," Calvin said with a wave. "You two have a good night."

Penelope fumbled her keys from her purse and opened the front door. "Get in here," she said, pulling him by the arm.

He grabbed his suitcase and wheeled it over the threshold.

"I was just having dinner with the Popes. Calvin invited me over at the last minute. Why didn't you call when you got here?"

"I didn't want to ruin the surprise. I saw your car was still here, so I figured you weren't far away. I've only been here a few minutes." Joey pulled her toward him and kissed her. "It was nice of Calvin to see you home."

"They're very good to me," Penelope said.

"I'm glad you're not too lonely out here without me," Joey said.

"Well," Penelope said, "you know I'd rather be home with you."

She motioned him to follow her to the kitchen where she grabbed two bottles of water from the refrigerator.

"How did you get here?"

"Uber from the airport," Joey said, taking one of the waters from her. "I'm very resourceful."

"I know this about you," Penelope said with a smile. "Are you hungry?"

"No," Joey said, twisting off the cap. "I grabbed a sandwich at the airport." He took a drink, then set the water down and pulled her to him again. "I am ready for bed, though. Cross country flying can wear a guy out."

"I bet," Penelope said with a smile. "Let's go up." She took his hand and led him upstairs.

CHAPTER 6

"When did you get a cat?" Joey asked the next morning over coffee.

"What are you talking about? I don't have a cat," Penelope said, following his gaze.

Joey tilted his mug at the sliding glass door. Mirabella sat on the other side, staring through the glass at them.

"Oh no," Penelope said. "She's gotten out again. The Popes will be looking for her."

"She doesn't look like an outside cat," Joey said. "Way too groomed. And is that a diamond on her collar?"

"You are a good detective," Penelope teased. She walked over and slid the door open. Mirabella stepped daintily inside, like she was returning home after a morning promenade around the pool and was ready for her breakfast. "And you're right, she's not an outside cat." Mirabella's soft fur brushed her ankles. "But judging from how often she shows up here, maybe she'd like to be."

"She likes you," Joey said, looking down at the purring fuzz ball. "Hey, don't they have coyotes out here? I'd be afraid one of them would try to eat her for breakfast if she were my cat."

"Coyotes?" Penelope said, alarmed. "I've never seen one around here, but I've been told they live in the area." She scooped Mirabella up from the ground and nuzzled her to her neck. "Don't you dare get eaten by a big bad wolf, you little cutie."

The doorbell rang.

"I'll get it," Joey said, pushing himself from the counter where he'd been leaning. They were both still in their pajamas, so Penelope was happy he was there to answer the door.

"Sorry to be a bother, but have you seen my cat?" The sound of Brogan's soft voice drifted down the front hallway. Her accent sounded more pronounced this morning.

"Your mom's come to get you," Penelope whispered to the cat, who purred loudly in her arms. "You're probably going to get grounded."

"I can't believe she's still mad about being boarded," Brogan said, striding into the living room on her short legs. She wore a kimono-style robe that fell to her knees over black leggings and workout top, her tan stomach peeking out, her tiny feet bare. "I was doing yoga in the bedroom upstairs and she leapt off the balcony into the palm tree next to the pool. Can you believe it? She's never done anything like that before." Brogan was breathless, like she had sprinted over from the main house.

"Oh my goodness," Penelope said. "So she's an acrobat? Who knew she had so many talents."

Brogan shook her head in frustration. "I'm so sorry. Hi, Joey."

Joey smiled. "Nice to see you again. Can I get you a cup of coffee?"

Brogan shook her head. "No thanks, I've cut out caffeine."

"We're always happy to have a visit from Mirabella," Penelope said, "but I'd hate for her to get hurt or lost."

Brogan took her cat and hugged her to her chest. "She might look fragile, but this little girl is fierce. She knows how to take care of herself."

"I'm so glad Penelope has such nice neighbors," Joey said. "It's made her being so far away from home a little easier."

"We can be nice," Brogan said. "Mostly me. I'm the nice one. And I know what it's like to be far away from home, too."

Joey glanced at Penelope and took a sip of his coffee.

"How long are you staying in town this time? We'll have to have you over for a barbeque," Brogan asked. Mirabella purred loudly and nuzzled her wiry neck.

"Two weeks or so," Joey said. "We'd like that, right, Penny?"

"Great," Brogan said, without waiting for her to answer. "I'll have Jacque put something together for the barbie. Maybe next week."

"I would've thought you'd be fast asleep," Penelope said. "You're handling the jetlag very well."

Brogan shrugged. "Jetlag is just a state of mind. I never understood why people are so affected. You just have to hydrate and take your vitamins before you fly, then take a nap on the plane. No worries at all." Her accent was faint, but it clipped through certain words when she spoke quickly, like she was at the moment.

"Anyway, I'll let the two of you get back to your morning. I know you have to get to the set soon, don't you, Penelope? Calvin's about to head into the studio." She stroked Mirabella's fur, which was the same deep black as Brogan's own hair, this morning unrestrained by a scarf or rubber band. It frizzed out around her petite head in wavy tendrils, in a wild natural look. Brogan reminded Penelope of a porcelain doll with her smooth cheeks and bowed lips.

"Yes, I need to get ready for work," Penelope said with a tinge of disappointment. "Back to the cliffs." She was reluctant to head out and leave Joey behind, who she realized she'd been missing more than she had admitted to herself. "Thanks for coming to get Mirabella. I hope she stops trying to fly out of windows."

Brogan gave Penelope a sweet smile and headed for the door, Joey trailing behind to see her out.

"That's California living for you," Penelope said. "Morning yoga with free range aerial cats."

"I think I could get used to it out here," Joey said with a wink. "Let's get a house in Salacia Beach, Penny. Who needs the cold Jersey winters anyway? I could join the local police force. Or sign up for the beach patrol."

Penelope laughed and rolled her eyes. "That could be a plan. Tell you what, let's think about it and talk again over dinner. I do love it here, but the houses might be slightly out of our price range. Especially the ones right on the ocean."

Joey went to her and looped his arms over her shoulders. "We can afford anything we want to have."

"Sure," Penelope said, circling his waist with her arms. "We can relocate three thousand miles away from home, no problem. We'll look for a place later. But right now I need a shower."

"Call in sick," Joey said, tugging her closer, continuing the playful game. "They won't miss you, not at all."

"That's tempting, but yes they would miss me," Penelope laughed.

"Not as much as I'll miss you," Joey murmured.

"I'll be back before you know it. Let's hope it's an easy day."

CHAPTER 7

Back on location on the cliffs, Penelope caught herself smiling while setting up brunch for the cast and crew, thinking about Joey back at the house. He offered to come with her to work, but she urged him to take the day off and relax, go for a swim in the ocean or do some reading out by the pool. He quickly agreed that her idea was the better one.

Because it was past breakfast time, but a little too early for lunch when their first scheduled break would take place, Penelope and her crew opted to put on brunch for the cast and crew.

"Can I have a Bloody Mary, then? Light on the horseradish and heavy on the vodka," Sebastian said with a wink as Penelope set out a pitcher of chilled tomato juice on the drinks station.

"Sorry, Chad hasn't authorized alcohol on the set today," Penelope said with a laugh. "Maybe when we wrap, whenever that will be. I can make you a mocktail version if you like."

Sebastian twisted his lips into a half frown. "Nah," he sighed. "My policy is to not mess with virgins...drinks or otherwise."

Penelope looked back down at her pitcher, ignoring his joke as she arranged lemon slices on a plate.

"Besides, I don't want to be puffy around the eyes tomorrow. We've got more days to go on this cliff, if my guess is right."

"Do tomatoes make you cry?" Penelope asked.

"Ha," Sebastian said. "No, darling. Salt is the enemy when your goal is looking lean on film. Tomato juice has tons of sodium."

"Not this kind," Penelope said. "It's fresh from our juicer."

"Still," Sebastian looked at the pitcher doubtfully.

"Right," Penelope said. "So, you don't think you'll be able to get this scene in the can today?"

"Probably not, considering our wonder boy director," Sebastian said.

Penelope deflated a bit. The cliff overlooking the ocean was definitely not the worst location she'd worked on, but she worried about the rest of the crew fatiguing from running through the same five minutes of script more than a few days in a row.

"Maybe everyone can pull together and finish it up," she said hopefully.

Sebastian shrugged. "It's not me who's holding things up, love. It's the persnickety man in charge." He picked up a cucumber slice from the vegetable tray on the table and popped it in his mouth.

"You can put those on your eyes too, you know," Penelope said. "To reduce swelling, if you decide to indulge in salt after all."

Sebastian snorted a laugh and ate another one. "I'll keep that in mind."

"I know it's none of my business," Penelope ventured. "I'm just the chef, but maybe if you listened to Chad instead of challenging him constantly...maybe you'd both be happier. You know, more like a collaboration. In the kitchen everyone has to work together or nothing makes it onto the plate."

Sebastian froze and eyed Penelope for a beat, his gaze

dropping from her eyes to study the line of her jaw, then back up again. She decided she'd overstepped and would not be offering any more advice to actors in the future during that uncomfortable moment of silence.

"You know," Sebastian said. "I think you may be right, wise chef. A kitchen brigade is the perfect example of teamwork."

Penelope smiled. "I was just thinking—"

"No," Sebastian interrupted. "You're right, Penelope. My acting coach is always saying I need to work on my listening skills, and that I should respect the views of others. Thank you for the reminder."

"Oh," Penelope said, surprised. "You're welcome."

"Everyone back to one," Chad called from his seat under the director's tent.

"Have a good day," Sebastian said as he strolled away.

Sebastian and Isaac took their places while members of the makeup and wardrobe teams shuffled around them, brushes and lint rollers buzzing. One of the prop handlers strolled over, handed Isaac the gun, then hustled out of the scene as Chad began counting down to action. A boom mike was lowered over their heads just out of camera range while three camera operators on steady-cam trolleys circled the men, ready to roll film when Chad called action. One of the PAs waved the digital scene marker board in front of the camera, noting it was the twenty-seventh take of the scene. Penelope tucked a tendril of loose hair back behind her ear.

Javier stepped down from the kitchen truck with three sauté pans in each hand and headed toward Penelope in the prep tent. She had asked him and Trevor, her other local chef, to set up an omelet station for the first break. She tossed them a glance, putting a finger to her lips. Javier nodded and they worked quietly on getting the omelet station set up. Her crew knew to keep noise to a minimum at all times during filming, but to be totally quiet when the actors were working. That was especially true on this set, where Chad had shown he could blow up at any moment. A few days ago a bird had cawed over their heads and Chad called cut to reset the entire scene, even though Penelope was pretty sure the sound editor could remove a noise like that in post production.

"I told you to let this go, little brother," Sebastian bellowed in the now familiar dialogue. "You don't understand. I have to find the killer."

Penelope recited the scripted words to herself as she wiped condensation from the side of the water pitcher and tied a linen napkin around it to manage the drips.

"And I'll keep hunting you and him," Isaac responded as he pointed the gun at Sebastian's chest.

"You don't have it in you to chase me down," Sebastian responded, taunting Isaac. Penelope heard Javier mumble the line under his breath behind her and suppressed a smile.

"I will chase you down until the end of time," Penelope heard in her head, and then from Isaac's mouth. She wondered if this movie was going to live up to the hype it had been getting. She knew she was only seeing pieces of it, the raw material, but to her it seemed like a lot of other films she'd seen, not remarkable, at least not in the dialogue.

A loud cracking sound came from the gun. It was jarring and caused Penelope to topple over the water pitcher she'd been wrapping a napkin around. The gunshot rang in her ears as she watched the ice water spill over the table and onto the sandy ground beneath the table.

The echo of the shot was still in the air when Chad jumped up from his seat and stood at the edge of his tent, his mouth hanging open.

The gun had never sounded like that before. In every other take it had been a weak pop, like a firecracker or a child's toy pistol.

Penelope lifted her gaze from the pool of ice water at her feet to the men near the cliff. Sebastian was on the ground, one hand brushing at his shirt, like he was trying to knock off a bug or a piece of lint. Bright red blood was spreading slowly across the white fabric, that was singed around the edges of a bullet hole. Isaac stood over him, staring at the gun in his hand.

"Medic!" Chad shouted. "We need a medic!"

Penelope grabbed a stack of cloth napkins and pushed aside the table in front of her, leaping around it and hurrying toward Sebastian. She fell to her knees at his side and pressed them to his chest. Chad knelt down beside her and helped apply pressure to the wound.

"Get it off of me," Sebastian said weakly. "It's burning."

"You're going to be okay," Penelope said firmly.

"Off...get it off," Sebastian said hoarsely.

"We need to try and stop the bleeding," Chad mumbled.

"What is happening?" Isaac shouted from behind them. He was still holding the gun, his eyes wild and glassy with tears.

The medic hurried over and knelt down on the other side of Sebastian. "Keep the pressure on," he directed Penelope as he yanked open his first aid kit and began sorting through the items inside. When he pulled out his phone and dialed 911 she could see his hands were shaking.

"We need an ambulance." He spoke calmly, although his hands continued to shake. "Salacia beach, off Highway One in North Cove. Gunshot, adult male, chest wound. We need help right away."

Sebastian looked at Penelope with an unfocused gaze.

"You're going to be okay," she said. "Help is on the way."

His eyelids drooped and he began to nod off.

"Stay awake. Sebastian," Penelope urged. "Stay with us."

The medic pressed a finger to his neck as more blood seeped through the napkins under Penelope's hand. She pressed harder, trying her best to stop the flow of blood.

A siren sounded in the distance.

"They're almost here," Penelope said. "You're going to be okay."

Chad sat motionless next to her.

"What happened?" Isaac said weakly, his face wet from tears. "Oh God, what have I done?"

CHAPTER 8

Penelope stumbled toward the catering tent, her legs rubbery and full of pins and needles from crouching on the ground next to Sebastian for so long. Her forearms ached from holding them rigid against Sebastian's chest for more than ten minutes until the ambulance arrived.

One of the paramedics firmly but gently moved her aside and took her spot, assessing the hole in Sebastian's chest. His partner applied a bandage to the wound and then they together loaded him onto a gurney. Sebastian had lost consciousness right before the ambulance pulled up at the edge of the road. She watched the paramedics rush Sebastian to the ambulance, one of them hopping in back with him, and the other hurrying to the driver's side door. The ambulance peeled away from the lot, speeding back toward town, sirens blaring.

Penelope's hands shook and she looked down, seeing that she still grasped the bloody napkins. Setting them down on the nearest table, she stepped inside, almost tripping over Javier, who was huddled on the ground, hugging his knees to his chest.

Penelope collapsed onto a chair next to him. "Javier, are you okay?"

His dark brown skin had paled to a sickly green color and he shivered all over. His short dark hair was slicked to his head and the neck of his chef coat was wet from sweating. He stared at the table legs in front of him, and didn't seem to notice her there.

"Javier," Penelope said softly.

His body jerked and he came back around, appearing confused for a second before focusing on her face. "Yes?"

"Are you okay?" Penelope repeated. Her voice sounded too loud in her ears, and had taken on an uncharacteristically shakiness.

Javier shook his head once, then nodded slowly. Trevor and Francis were standing in front of the kitchen truck talking closely and shaking their heads. Penelope called to them and waved them over.

"Can you get up?" she said quietly to Javier.

The color had begun to return to his face and he pushed himself up with the help of the table behind him. A police car pulled into the lot and parked behind the kitchen truck. A pair of uniformed officers emerged and walked toward Chad and Isaac, who were standing near where Sebastian had fallen. The taller one approached Isaac cautiously and motioned for the stunned actor to hand him the gun. He almost tossed it at the cop, almost like he'd forgotten he was holding it.

"What happened, Boss?" Trevor asked, eyeing the police.

"Sebastian is..." Penelope began. "Something went wrong with the prop gun."

Javier took a few deep breaths and turned away from them, facing out toward the ocean.

"Let's stick together until we know what's going on," Penelope suggested. "I'm sure the police are going to have some questions. Think about what you were doing when the accident happened."

A dark sedan pulled into the lot and ground to a stop behind the cruiser. An older woman and a young man, both wearing dark suits and sunglasses emerged and headed toward where the other officers were talking to Chad and Isaac. Chad's expression was one Penelope hadn't seen before: fear and confusion.

Isaac walked on shaky legs after the detectives motioned for him to step inside the tent and take a seat next to Chad. The female detective glanced at Penelope and her team, then instructed Chad to gather the rest of the crew to join them inside. Isaac sat at a table behind Penelope and dropped his head into his hands.

"What's your name?"

Startled, Penelope turned, coming face to face with her partner.

"Sutherland," she said. "Sorry, Penelope."

The detective glanced at her hands and she followed his gaze, seeing a smear of blood on the hem of her apron.

"Are you hurt?" he asked. Several members of the camera crew filed past, staring wide eyed at her before finding their seats.

"No," Penelope said. "I'm just...trying to calm down." She was feeling a delayed sense of shock, and like she might cry at any second.

"I'm Detective Adalbert, that's my partner Detective Zahn," he said. "Can you tell me what happened?"

"Yes," Penelope said. "Well, sort of...I was working, getting things together for brunch, and they've done the scene so many times, and I've seen it so many times, so I wasn't paying that much attention..." She glanced down at the blood, aware she was rambling. She took a deep breath and slowed down. "I was listening to Sebastian and Isaac run through their lines and..." she paused, her words picking up speed again. The detective touched her lightly on the shoulder.

"It's okay," Adalbert said. "Take your time."

Penelope closed her eyes for a second, remembering. Her phone buzzed in her back pocket and she opened them again. Over Adalbert's shoulder, she could see Chad talking to Detective Zahn.

"Then there was a loud gunshot, and Sebastian was on the ground bleeding." Penelope rubbed at the smear of blood on her chef coat. "And then I ran over and...they took Sebastian away in the ambulance, and then you got here."

Adalbert nodded, his dark brown eyes searching her face. "Anything else you can remember?"

"Wait," Penelope said, scanning the tent. "Where's the prop handler?"

"The who?" Adalbert asked. His voice had a musical quality to it that was soothing.

"The prop handler," Penelope repeated. "The guy who handed Isaac the gun. I don't see him."

Adalbert looked at the cast and crew members that had gathered under the tent. "Are you sure? There's, like, a lot of people here..."

Penelope shook her head. "I remember because I hadn't seen him on the set before. Which isn't that unusual, it's a big studio and there are lots of projects going on, so we get people in and out of here. But I know I saw a guy hand Isaac the gun, and now...he's gone."

CHAPTER 9

Penelope retrieved her phone from her pocket after Detective Adalbert stepped away to confer with his partner. She had missed a call from Joey, and two from Calvin Pope. Adalbert and Zahn were now questioning Isaac. His eyes kept darting out toward the ocean whenever he paused to listen, his broad shoulders caving toward his chest.

Penelope's phone buzzed again and she looked at the screen.

"Hi, Calvin," she said quietly.

"Penelope, thank God," Calvin shouted. "Scarlett called. She got word from one of the PAs on the set about an accident involving Sebastian. What on earth happened? Chad's not answering his phone."

"Yes there was an incident," Penelope said. "Something went wrong with the prop gun and Sebastian was injured." Detective Adalbert was heading toward her and motioning her to lower her phone. "The police are here. They're questioning the crew."

"Was anyone else hurt?" Calvin asked, his voice a pitch higher than normal. Penelope held out her phone, offering it to the detective without answering. "It's Calvin Pope on the line, the producer of the film."

"Sir?" Adalbert said, taking the phone from Penelope and

turning away. "Where are you right now?" Penelope found herself listening to several conversations at once, overwhelmed by the activity around her. As Adalbert turned away, she focused on the one between Isaac and the other detective.

"You're sure the person that gave you the gun isn't here," Zahn said to Isaac.

He shook his head back and forth slowly. "I'm not even sure who handed it to me," Isaac said. "It was one of the prop guys. He didn't say anything, just gave it to me, stuck it in my hand."

"Did it feel any different from the other times you've held the gun?" Zahn asked.

Isaac shook his head again. "Not really, it's hard to say."

"Have you ever shot an actual gun before?"

"No," Isaac admitted. "I haven't held that many weapons at all, in real life at least."

"And you're sure you've never seen this man, this property clerk before?"

"I don't think so. We've had a few different prop handlers on this set. I don't think I've talked with any of them to be honest." He ducked his head and closed his eyes for a second.

Penelope's gaze traveled back to Javier, who appeared lost in thought, splayed across a chair, like he'd just finished running a marathon. She took a few steps closer to Isaac and Detective Zahn, and leaned into their conversation.

"He's definitely not here," Penelope mumbled, scanning the crowd in the tent.

"Okay," Zahn said with a sigh. "Can either of you remember what this prop handler was wearing? Any physical description?"

"I didn't even look at him," Isaac said. "I was thinking about the scene, my lines...I wasn't paying attention to the crew around me. There were makeup people, wardrobe, the script supervisor. A flurry of faces."

Penelope searched her memory, then said, "He was wearing jeans and a beige jacket, one of those heavy ones, like not denim but what farmers wear sometimes. Which is kind of weird considering how warm it can get up here."

"Was he wearing a baseball hat?" Isaac asked Penelope.

"Yes. Maybe a Dodgers hat," Penelope said.

"Hair and skin color?" Zahn asked.

"I think he was white, with brown hair maybe. I'm sorry, that's all I can remember. I didn't get a good look at his face."

"Okay," Zahn said with a sigh. "Did anyone else see this guy?"

Penelope waved to her team. Francis and Trevor walked over to them but Javier stayed in his chair. He had pulled himself up to a more normal seated position, but still looked exhausted.

"We were up in the truck," Francis said with a shrug. "I didn't see anything until after it happened." Trevor nodded in agreement.

"He had a black fingernail," Javier said. "They guy with the jacket."

Everyone turned to the cook who hadn't said much at all since the accident.

"You saw him up close? Close enough to see his hands?" Detective Adalbert pressed, stepping back inside the tent to join their conversation. He handed Penelope back her phone.

"I wasn't looking at him, really, but I always notice if people's hands are dirty when they're at the coffee station, touching the cups and things, in case I have to go behind and clean up after them. I think the guy in the brown jacket came to get a cup of coffee while they were setting up the tents. His thumbnail was black," Javier said.

"Like, painted black?" Adalbert asked.

"No, like he'd caught it in a door or something. Bruised black," Javier said. His eyes were unfocused, like he was reaching back into his memory. "Otherwise he acted totally normal. Black coffee, no sugar or cream."

"Make a note to secure all of the trash up here," Zahn said to her partner. "Maybe we get lucky with a print or some DNA."

Penelope looked around the tent. They'd put out paper coffee cups this morning as always, and the stacks were about half of what they were when they set up. Coffee was as important to movie sets as film itself, and she always made sure they had plenty brewing, all times of the day. She thought of it as creative fuel for the entire team. Chad entered the tent just as he was finishing up a phone call.

"We have trash receptacles set up in here," Penelope said. "And then there are cans in every trailer and in the mobile bathrooms."

Detective Zahn took notes as she spoke. "We'll collect them all. I mean, the guy could've taken the cup with him, if he was smart, but it can't hurt to look. Any news from the studio?" she asked Chad.

He shook his head. "The regular prop guy who was on the call sheet this morning got sent to another set, and the person who showed up here today signed in as the regular guy."

A quick look passed between the detectives, but no words were spoken. Penelope wondered how long they'd been working together to develop that kind of shorthand communication.

"So it couldn't have been an accident," Penelope said. "That's what that means, right?"

"How many cameras were rolling tape while you were setting up the shot?" Adalbert asked Chad, ignoring Penelope's question. "What's the chance we have this guy on film?"

Chad brushed the stubble on his chin. "I mean maybe, we'll

roll back tape from right before, but as a cost cutting measure, my guys don't roll film until I call action."

"Cost cutting, huh?" Zahn said. "What does this project cost, twenty million dollars?"

"Thirty-two," Chad mumbled. "About. More now, probably."

Detective Zahn shook her head slightly then cleared her throat. "I still want a look at all film from today, and the past few days. Anything of the crew, outtakes, you know what I'm asking for?"

Chad nodded and stood up.

"When I talked to the studio before they said they were gathering together everyone who had anything to do with this...film," Adalbert said to his partner after a glance at Penelope. "Think we should head over and get into the employee files?"

Detective Zahn sighed and scanned the crowd gathered under the tent. "Yeah. You stay here and get statements from everyone. I'll head to the studio and see what I can work on that end. And I'll take him in for processing." She lifted her chin at Isaac. At the sound of his name he snapped out of his daze and straightened up in the chair.

"Processed?" he said loudly. "You're arresting me? I didn't mean to shoot him."

Detective Zahn directed one of the uniformed officers to take Isaac into custody.

"You're under arrest on the charge of negligently discharging a firearm," Zahn said, rubbing the back of her neck with her thin long fingers.

"You can't arrest me," Isaac said, standing up. "I didn't do anything wrong. It was the prop guy! Go find him!"

"We have to bring you in," Zahn said, crossing her arms.

"We only have your word it was an accident, and it's the law. Until we find out exactly what happened, you're going to have to come with us."

CHAPTER 10

After they each gave official statements about what they'd witnessed that morning to the uniformed officers, Penelope and her team were allowed to clear everything down and head back to the warehouse studio.

While she was pulling down the awning of her kitchen truck and securing it for the drive back, Chad approached her, looking as emotionally wrung out as she did.

"I just wanted to say..." Chad began as Penelope spun the latches on her truck, locking the awning in place.

"What's that?" Penelope said over her shoulder after he stopped talking for a beat too long.

"You were great out there, you know...before," Chad said, a touch of awe in his voice. "Everyone froze but you jumped into action. It was...impressive."

"Oh," Penelope said. "I just did what anyone else would've done."

"That's the point. No one else did anything to help him," Chad said.

Penelope looked at the sandy ground and pushed down the bubble of emotion that wormed its way through her chest. The image of the ice water pooling around her feet crept into her mind, followed by a flash of the hole in Sebastian's chest.

"Anyway," Chad said, clearing his throat, "the bosses want

all the department heads in a meeting at the studio. Three o'clock."

"Catering too?" Penelope said. She'd really wanted to head home, back to Joey and away from the trauma she'd experienced that afternoon. She was weary, as if her limbs had been weighted down from the adrenalin rush she'd experienced right after the accident.

"They said everyone," Chad said. "You too."

"Okay," Penelope sighed. "Have there been any updates on Sebastian?"

Chad pinched the bridge of his nose and shook his head. "Not yet. Look, I know he and I have had our differences, and working together has been hard, but all I want right now is for him to sit up in that hospital bed and call me an incompetent jerk again."

Penelope reached out and squeezed his thin shoulder. "Keep a good thought," she said. "He's strong. I'm sure he'll be okay."

Chad smiled at her uncertainly and then headed for his tent without another word. She hoped Calvin wouldn't place too much blame on Chad's shoulders for what had happened that day.

Stepping inside the truck, Penelope saw her team huddled together talking quietly.

"We ready to roll?" she said, interrupting them.

"Please, let's get out of here," Trevor said. He'd wrapped a blue bandana around his head that helped contain his longish blond surfer hair. "It's been a terrible day for sure."

"Trevor, you drive the kitchen to home base today," she said. He nodded and hopped through the door back outside.

"I'll ride shotgun," Francis said, following him. He paused in the doorway and gave Penelope a concerned look, flicking his eyes to Javier who lingered by the grill, wiping at an imaginary spot next to the grate.

"We can ride together in the pantry truck," Penelope said. "You ready?" she added, looking at the immaculately polished spot he'd been rubbing.

Javier stopped rubbing and folded the kitchen towel into a neat square, setting it down on the counter. He tapped his knuckles on the metal and lifted his eyes to hers.

Penelope waited patiently, sensing that he was working up to something.

"I just wanted to say...ma'am," Javier began, staring back down at the shiny counter.

Penelope leaned against the opposite counter and waited for him to continue.

"I'm sorry I didn't help out there earlier," he said quietly. "I totally froze, and I know that's unacceptable. I wanted to apologize to you."

Penelope waited a few moments then said, "You don't have to apologize, Javier. What happened was totally unexpected. A real shooting on a set, for goodness sake. None of us knows what we'd do—"

"I should have been better," Javier said firmly. "I've been through combat training, active duty. I know exactly what I'm supposed to do in these situations. I did nothing. I failed everyone here."

"Javier, you're making too much of—"

"I don't expect you to understand," Javier interrupted.

"Well, help me to understand, then," Penelope said.

"I have PTSD," Javier said. "From my time serving as a combat cook."

"Oh," Penelope said at a loss for words. She'd read about Post Traumatic Stress Disorder many times, but hadn't met anyone who had experienced it and wasn't sure what she was supposed to say.

"It doesn't normally come up," Javier said. "But there are triggers."

"And witnessing a shooting would obviously be one of them," Penelope said. "Oh, Javier, I'm so sorry."

"Unexpected," Javier said. "It was all so unexpected."

"I remember from your résumé you cooked in the service, but you've never talked about it with me."

"I don't like to think about it. Well, I miss my friends, so it's nice to think about that part," Javier said. "I served in Afghanistan for two tours with the second battalion, eighth Marine regiment."

"That must have been hard," Penelope said.

"It's unlike anything I've ever seen," Javier said.

"Still, I don't think you should be so hard on yourself," Penelope said. "What happened today...I think a lot of people weren't sure how to react."

Javier smiled grimly. "You ran toward a man holding a gun without hesitation to help another one bleeding on the ground, maybe saving his life while I..." His eyes became shiny. "You know, I joined up with the service to get out of South LA, get a chance at something else, after my father was shot outside the restaurant he was working in. Right on the street, a drive-by. I wanted something more than what my uncles and brothers do to survive. I didn't want to sell drugs for a living. I thought at least over there, I'd know when the bullets were coming for me. I didn't count on everything else that happens...watching your friends die, losing people when you're not expecting it, watching them go out on a mission and never coming back."

Penelope listened, trying to imagine the things Javier had seen, and the dangerous harshness of his life at such a young age.

"Javier, I'm so glad you have survived. And that you're with us now. I can't tell you enough how much I appreciate you being here."

Javier picked up the towel again and started rubbing the same clean spot, avoiding her gaze.

"Let's head back," Penelope said. The truck's engine roared to life and the floor beneath their feet rumbled. "Today was...let's just put today behind us. Accidents happen on sets, and we just have to hope for the best, keep Sebastian in our prayers."

Javier laughed harshly. "I've seen a lot of people get shot, Boss. Dozens of them. Never once was it an accident."

Penelope bit her bottom lip, then motioned for him to follow her out of the kitchen truck. She'd seen way fewer people get shot than Javier had, and she hoped it wasn't something she'd ever witness again.

CHAPTER 11

When they arrived back at the studio, Penelope asked her team to put anything that needed to be refrigerated away in the kitchen, then met them again in the parking lot next to the truck.

"Get some rest," she'd said, paying particular attention to Javier. Trevor seemed back to his usual carefree self, while Francis looked exhausted. Javier still seemed jumpy, but he was much more relaxed than he was an hour earlier out on the cliffs.

After seeing them off and making sure the hatch and doors of the kitchen truck were locked and secure, Penelope headed back inside.

Calvin had built the Pope Productions studio in one of the remodeled fish canning factories that had dotted the shoreline back in the early 1900s. To the left of the entrance on the second floor were glass encased offices where the Pope executives and office staff worked. Calvin's suite was in the back corner and was flanked by the junior executive offices on either side, including Scarlett's. The first-floor space was dedicated to multiple sets and sound stages that could be transformed into any interior shot they needed for the various TV shows and films that were filmed here. Today the sets were quiet, which added an eerie quality to the building. Normally there would be at least one production crew buzzing around the sets, but today it was like a

Sunday afternoon, as quiet as a church.

The studio's industrial kitchen sat at the back of the first floor, complete with an adjoining office, which was where Penelope had been working. There was also a gym with an attached spa, wardrobe suites, and a long row of hair and makeup chairs, all currently vacant. Penelope listened to the soles of her shoes squeak against the sealed concrete floors as she made her way through the kitchen to the locker rooms behind.

She always kept a spare set of clothes in her office, which came in handy on a couple of occasions when she'd spilled something or it had been a sweaty day on the set and she felt like changing. It was nice that the studio offered a place for the crew to shower. Penelope had never worked out of a large studio before, and she'd enjoyed the different amenities one could offer. Her kitchen was state of the art, with large walk-in ovens, bigger than she'd ever seen or used before, and every kitchen appliance she'd ever heard of at her disposal.

Moving to Salacia Beach could be nice. She thought back to her conversation with Joey that morning, his half serious, half joking suggestion that they relocate together. Penelope had managed to put off buying a house with Joey in New Jersey. She really wanted to start a new chapter with him but when this opportunity came up, she couldn't pass it up. Joey had taken it in stride, in his ever-supportive kind of way. But she knew he'd want to make the next step soon, and they were arriving at that particular fork in the road.

Penelope slid off her blood-stained chef coat, stuffing it into her gym bag on the wooden bench next to her locker. Standing in front of one of the sinks, she turned on the water and looked in the mirror. A faint smear of dried blood brushed her jawline, and a few flecks dotted her neck just above her collar. Tilting her head she turned on the water and dabbed it off with wet fingers, then grabbed a towel from the dispenser and gently wiped at the spots.

She remembered Sebastian's eyes locking onto hers, and the faraway look she saw as he started to fade. Penelope closed her eyes and sent him a healing thought, then wondered about his family. She'd never heard him talk about anyone back home, and had only ever seen stories about Sebastian dating a series of models, all with names that were unfamiliar to Penelope. But surely Sebastian had parents back home, a mother who might have gotten some very upsetting news today.

Penelope tossed the paper towel in the bin and turned her thoughts to Isaac. He seemed bewildered after the gun went off. So much had been happening in the moments right after the accident. He certainly appeared to be upset as the officers led him away from the scene.

Then there was Chad, who had gotten to Sebastian's side as quickly as she had. He'd always come across as passive and weak somehow, but Penelope had revised her opinion of him that afternoon. He'd taken charge and had helped Sebastian as much as any of them could.

Penelope pulled off her shirt and replayed the scene over in her mind, trying to remember more about the prop handler. She felt like she was good with faces and had a sharp memory, but with all of the different people milling about on a movie set day after day, there were times when the faces of her coworkers began to blend together. Unable to come up with more details about the man, apart from the ones she'd already told the detectives, she sighed and pulled a fresh t-shirt from her locker and stuffed the soiled one into her gym bag.

*   *   *

In the large conference room fifteen minutes later, Penelope leaned against the wall, surrounded by the other supervisors and department heads on the film. Calvin sat at the head of the long table with Scarlett at his side. The rest of the chairs were occupied by different executives from Pope Productions, a few of them familiar, but a couple Penelope hadn't worked with before. She tapped her toe on the floor while they waited for everyone to get settled.

"I know you all have questions about what happened today," Calvin began. "And I've asked you all here to update you and discuss what happens next with *Severed Lives*."

An anxious silence fell across the room as all attention was directed to him. Chad sat to his right, his clothes rumpled and his face haggard. He kept his eyes on the table in front of him.

"We're very close to the end of principal filming—" Chad began.

"I don't want to hear from you yet," Calvin said, cutting him off. "This never would've happened if you'd stayed on schedule in the first place. You not only cost me money but now...I can't even look at you."

Chad stared at Calvin, his mouth hanging open. The rest of the people around the table shifted uncomfortably in their seats.

"Mr. Pope." The desk phone on the table in front of Calvin lit up and a woman's voice broke the silence. He pressed a button and responded. "Yes?"

"An urgent call. You said to put them through before—"

Cutting her off, he picked up the receiver. "Who is it?" he snapped. "Yes, okay, put the call through." Scarlett studied his face as he listened, her expression more angry than concerned, it seemed to Penelope.

Calvin listened to the person on the other end, his eyes roving around the room at the others. When they came to Penelope they stopped, and he stared at her as he said, "Okay, thanks for letting us know." He set the phone down carefully and set his elbows down on the table, leaning forward.

"I'm sorry to inform you all that Sebastian Beauregard didn't survive his injuries," Calvin said. "They tried everything they could but he's...he passed away during surgery."

"Dead?" Chad said in a loud voice. "Sebastian's dead?"

Calvin dropped his head into his hands. Scarlett jotted something on the pad of paper on the table in front of her.

Penelope felt a wave of exhaustion hit her and for a moment felt like she could no longer stand. Her knees buckled and she pressed her back against the wall to support herself.

"What happens now?" one of the executives asked.

"The press is going to be all over this thing," another chimed in.

"What about the production?" more than one person added.

Calvin held up a hand until everyone fell silent again. "We'll designate someone from communications to talk to the press. I don't want anyone in this room to speak to a reporter or blogger, or God help you post anything on social media about what happened today. After we, meaning Pope Productions," he glanced at his daughter before continuing, "take a day or two to mourn the loss of one of our own, we'll decide what to do about everything else."

"We've spent close to thirty million dollars on this movie. We can't afford to not finish principal filming," Scarlett said.

Calvin glared at her. Scarlett did not shrink from his gaze, instead she set her jaw in a hard line as if challenging him to disagree with her.

"First we mourn, then we talk business," he said to his daughter. "We have not lost all decency, not yet. I don't care how much it costs."

Scarlett's expression softened slightly, but her jaw remained granite hard.

"Everyone out," Calvin said wearily. "Except you." He pointed at Chad with his thick finger. "You hated Sebastian, and got us into this mess. You are going to help me figure out how to end this disaster. The rest of you go home. Mourn on your own time."

The room cleared out, with only the sound of chairs scraping across the polished concrete floor accompanying the mumbled whispers from the executive team. Penelope stayed put as the group filed past Calvin, throwing him cautious glances as they went. Scarlett was the last to stand, and left him sitting there without a word.

After Scarlett cleared the doorway Penelope said, "You're not going to be able to stop people from talking about what happened today. There were a lot of crew members up on that cliff this morning." Chad stared stonily at the wall opposite of where he sat.

Calvin grimaced and nodded. "I know. I just don't want it to come from someone on the executive team."

Penelope headed for the door. "I'll tell the guys, for what it's worth. I don't think any of them would talk to the media, but I'll be sure to mention that they shouldn't."

"You have no idea what people will do," Calvin said darkly. "A story like this...there will be financial offers made from the press, people will sell what they saw, offer pictures from their own phones. It always happens."

Penelope shrugged. "Considering a man has lost his life today...all of that seems pretty unimportant."

Calvin gave her a fiery glance as she paused in the doorway. "Money makes people behave in ways where you wouldn't even recognize them. Trust me, I know." He looked at Chad and shook his head.

"Sometimes people can surprise you by being decent human beings," she said as she left, not waiting for a response.

CHAPTER 12

"Are you okay?" Joey was waiting for her on the front porch when Penelope got home. "I've been watching the news reports about the accident on the set."

"I'll be fine," she said. "So the media already has the story? I don't want to watch any of it yet."

"They're not saying much," Joey said. "Just reporting that an actor died, and the general location where it happened. Come on, sit down." Joey led her into the living room and turned off the TV. She sat on the sofa in front of the fireplace, and he knelt down to untie her shoes. He slipped them gently off her feet.

"Calvin is blaming Chad for some reason," Penelope said. "I mean, he and Sebastian didn't get along, but it was just work stuff. I don't think Chad hated Sebastian enough to set him up to get shot."

Joey sat down on the floor in front of her and put her feet in his lap. "Did they ever get physical with each other?"

"No," Penelope said with a weak laugh. "Chad weighs a hundred and fifty pounds soaking wet. Sebastian looked like Mr. Universe with his shirt off."

"Really," Joey said tensely.

"You know what I mean," Penelope said. "It wouldn't be much of a fight if they did, is what I'm saying."

"I know," Joey said soothingly.

"I've never watched anyone…" Penelope began, then trailed off. Joey kneaded the pad of her right foot with his strong hands. "I've never seen that happen to anyone before, witnessed someone dying."

"It's not something you ever want to get used to," Joey said.

"I can't imagine how you handle it, Joey," Penelope said. "The violence you see every day."

"Well," Joey said, setting down her foot and easing up her other one. "It's not a constant day to day thing. But yeah, it's awful to see what people are capable of sometimes."

Penelope focused on his firm yet gentle grip, feeling the tension seep away from his touch. "I'm so tired," she said, drifting.

"Here," Joey said, standing up. "Lie down."

Penelope stretched out on the couch. Joey eased a pillow under her head and shook out the blanket that was draped over the back, laying it on top of her and tucking it around her feet. Penelope was asleep by the time he walked over to the sliding glass door to ease the curtains closed.

Penelope woke over an hour later to the sound of the refrigerator door opening. Sitting up groggily she saw Joey in the kitchen, leaning his arm on the door of the fridge surveying the contents.

"Hey," Penelope said. Her mouth was dry and her head still heavy from sleep.

"You're up," Joey said, turning toward her. "How are you feeling?"

"Tired," Penelope said. "How long have I been asleep?"

"A little while," Joey said. He poured her a glass of water from a pitcher and brought it to the couch. She accepted it gratefully and took a long sip. "Adrenaline crashes will do that to you."

Penelope nodded and set the water down on the coffee table in front of the couch.

"They're still reporting on what happened," Joey said, sitting down next to her. Penelope leaned into him and he draped an arm over her shoulder, pulling her close. "Sebastian's death, the shooting."

"I knew they would be," Penelope said.

"The other guy, the suspect I guess, they haven't named him, but the reports are that it was an accidental shooting on the set of an upcoming film."

"That's what happened," Penelope said. "What do you think of them charging Isaac, though? I mean if it was an accident…"

"Well," Joey said, "even in an accidental shooting charges can be brought. Most of the time it's a firearms violation, or a negligence charge."

"I think that's what the detective on the set called it," Penelope said, reaching for her water again. "Negligence."

"Yeah, they're going to hold him on something," Joey said, "until they determine without a doubt it was really an accident."

Penelope took another sip of water. "But if you're going to shoot someone on purpose, would you do it in front of over seventy witnesses?"

"I might," Joey said, "if I wanted everyone to think I didn't really mean to do it. Who knows? This Isaac guy might have thought he'd commit the perfect murder in broad daylight."

Penelope shook her head. "No, it's the prop guy who handed Isaac the gun then disappeared afterwards. That's who the police should be looking for. Isaac and Sebastian got along great, were friends even. I never picked up on any tension between them at all on the set and I know they hung out together. I'm pretty sure Sebastian recommended Isaac for the role of his brother, because they'd worked together in the past."

"How did this prop guy just walk on and off the set without anyone noticing?" Joey asked.

Penelope shrugged. "It would be easy enough to slip in and out, then head to the parking area without anyone seeing. There were at least forty vehicles there when we parked. He probably drove himself there and left the same way."

"But how did this guy get onto the set and pose as a member of the crew? Don't you have a way of knowing who is working on a location?"

"Yes. Well, technically we do," Penelope said. "Everyone is supposed to sign in at the production office first, and then we caravan to wherever we're filming that day. I can see where someone could slip in and out though. It's not like we're under armed guard. It would be easy enough to pose as the member of the crew."

"And how does it work getting assigned to a specific location?"

"What do you mean?" Penelope asked.

"I'm assuming this guy doesn't work for...what's it called?"

"The studio, Pope Productions," Penelope said.

"Right," Joey said.

"The studio has several different projects going on at the same time," Penelope said, following his train of thought. "So this guy either used the name of another employee..."

"Or it's someone who already works there," Joey said. "They're probably tracking this guy down as we speak. That's what I'd be doing as lead detective."

"I wish I could remember more about him," Penelope said. "I only have a vague memory of a totally unremarkable guy walking up to Isaac."

"I think that's enough for today," Joey said, lifting her chin with his finger and kissing her gently on the lips. "Let's leave what happened today alone for now. I don't know about you, but I'm starving. And I'm cooking tonight."

"I'm so glad you're here to help me through this," Penelope said, after another kiss. "And you making dinner sounds perfect."

CHAPTER 13

The next day after a leisurely lie in and breakfast, Penelope and Joey decided to spend the rest of the morning relaxing by the pool. Side by side in two of the lounge chairs, Penelope read the news on her iPad while Joey closed his eyes and let the sun warm his face. There was nothing new reported than what she'd known about the case the day before. No other suspects had been uncovered, and Isaac had been arrested for negligent discharge of a firearm.

"They're still investigating," Penelope murmured. "No new information yet."

"The press doesn't always report everything," Joey reminded her. "They release limited information, things that help the investigation that the police department gives them. The reputable press anyway. It's a tricky relationship at times, between us and them."

Penelope continued to read as they listened to the waves crashing rhythmically on the beach below. "It's going to feel strange going back in to work after all of this," she said. "I have to admit when I got the text this morning calling us back tomorrow, I felt a little queasy."

"It does seem a little soon," Joey said. "But I guess the show must go on, as they say."

"Yeah," Penelope said with a sigh. "I think if we weren't so close to the end of filming maybe things would be different. We'd might get a few more days off to adjust. I'm sure they want to push through to the end and let everyone go. Most of the crew have lined up jobs after this one, so it will be good to be done, to move onto other projects."

"What about you? What are you going to do next?" Joey asked.

"I'm supposed to be consulting on this new TV show for Calvin and Scarlett," Penelope said. "The culinary one, remember?"

"Yes," Joey said. "They're still moving forward on that?"

Penelope shrugged. "I assume so. I haven't heard any differently."

"And then you're coming home," Joey said with a smile. "Unless you really want to stay out here."

"I can't wait to get home," Penelope said. "And spend a lot of time with you."

"And restart our house search?" Joey asked. His hands cradled his head and his eyes were hidden behind his reflective sunglasses.

"I thought you wanted a beach house out here," Penelope said with a sly grin.

"Any house, as long as you're in it," Joey said, becoming serious, "is where I want to live."

A door slammed somewhere behind them, and loud shouting jerked them from their blissful moment. Joey tensed next to her but kept his eyes closed and his face tilted toward the sun. Calvin and Brogan were arguing behind the glass wall of their house, their voices raised but muffled.

"Can you hear them?" Penelope asked.

"Shh," Joey said. "Just ignore them. It's none of our business."

The two voices became clearer after Penelope heard the swooshing sound of the sliding glass door being yanked open and rattling on its track.

"Get back in here," Calvin said. His voice was raised to a level Penelope hadn't heard before, his words choked with anger.

"I've always known you had a cold heart," Brogan shouted. "But this is ridiculous. I'm fed up with the way you treat people."

Penelope sat up in her lounge chair. Joey put a hand on her arm and held it tightly, urging her to stay put. "It's none of our business," he quietly repeated.

Penelope eased back down but the relaxed feeling she had been enjoying had slipped away, the tension causing her shoulders to creep up toward her ears.

"You're just going to go on making your stupid movie like nothing ever happened. Like Sebastian didn't just die right there in front of everyone!" Brogan shouted. "He was a real person. Not some object you can swap out like a department store mannequin."

"I'm done discussing this with you," Calvin said. "I know you were friends with Sebastian, but I can't pull the plug on the project and lose all of that money."

"You could take more than one day to…to mourn his loss," Brogan said, her voice pleading.

"I'm not going to get into the finer points of film finance with you, a faded wannabe soap opera star from New Zealand," Calvin said sarcastically.

"It always comes down to money with you," Brogan said sharply.

"Look who's talking," Calvin retorted. "What's wrong, your allowance not big enough again? If you would actually work for a living, you'd know the value of a dollar."

"That's hilarious, coming from you," Brogan spat. "Spoiled rich brat."

"My dear, you wouldn't know a hard day's work if it walked up to you and introduced itself. And I wasn't spoiled."

"Yes, you are spoiled. And you have no feelings whatsoever in that cold dark heart," Brogan screamed.

"I won't have you tell me my business," Calvin warned. "The fact that you'd come out here and make a scene like this...just proves you're..."

"I'm what?" Brogan retorted.

"Not worth it," Calvin muttered.

"I'm worth more than you know," Brogan challenged.

"That's not what I mean," Calvin countered. "I mean this conversation isn't worth my breath."

"That's not what you meant," Brogan shouted.

"This is getting really ugly," Penelope whispered. Joey shook his head slightly and put a finger to his lips.

"Don't test me, Brogan," Calvin said. "You wouldn't like to see how far I'll go."

"Oh I know how far you can go. I'm not going to just go take a swim like the last one," Brogan said. "It will take more than that for you to get rid of me."

There was silence for what felt like a full minute and Penelope thought the argument between the Popes was over. She glanced at Joey who was so still she wondered if he'd drifted off to sleep.

Footsteps crunched on the gravel right on the other side of the wall and Penelope held her breath. She heard what sounded like kissing coming from the other side. Penelope's mouth fell open. How could Calvin and Brogan kiss after a blowup like that?

"Come back inside," Calvin said, his voice calm and gravely.

The next thing they heard were retreating footsteps and the glass door sliding closed.

When she was sure the Popes were no longer within earshot, Penelope said, "What in the heck was that?"

"An argument between a husband and wife," Joey said, keeping his voice low. A trickle of sweat slid down from his neck, dampening the dark hair on his chest. His skin was turning pink in the morning sun. Penelope sat up and grabbed a bottle of sunscreen from her bag on the ground and opened it.

"That was some disagreement," Penelope said. "And how could they have made up so quickly after those...things they said?"

"Don't judge. Every marriage is different," Joey advised. "We have no idea what goes on behind closed doors, and I have a feeling most of the time we wouldn't want to know."

"You're right," Penelope said with a sigh. "We've never argued like that."

"We're not married," Joey reminded her.

"Do you think it makes that much difference?" Penelope asked.

Joey shrugged. "I think it probably does. But I can't imagine us ever going at it like that, can you?"

Penelope laughed, the tension easing. "Maybe if you tried to tell me how to cook, or tried to take over the kitchen at home without my input."

"See?" Joey said, "I would never do that. We're going to excel at marriage." He sat up on his chaise and Penelope rubbed some sunscreen onto his chest for him.

"Are you proposing right now?" Penelope joked as she rubbed some lotion on his shoulders.

"I've been thinking about how to propose to you for a long time, Penny Blue," Joey said. The jovial tone of his voice was gone, and he sounded dead serious.

Penelope's cheeks reddened and she focused on his other shoulder. He took the bottle of lotion from her hand and squirted some into his palm, and motioned for her to turn around. She did and he gently applied some sunscreen to her back and shoulders. "I have to get my timing right," he said. "Make sure you're in a yes mood first."

Penelope laughed. "Okay, well, you'll let me know, right?"

"Yes," Joey said. "When the time is just right."

They settled back on their chaises and were quiet for a few minutes, listening to the waves crash on the beach below.

"I suppose what happened on the set must be really upsetting and stressful for Calvin. And Sebastian and Brogan were friends. So they're both not themselves right now."

Joey made a sympathetic noise in response.

"Everyone deals with stress differently," Penelope continued. She was still thinking about the argument they'd overheard. "What do you suppose Brogan was talking about when she said she wasn't going to take a swim like the other one?"

"You got me," Joey said. "Maybe it's a New Zealand saying, like when you tell someone to go jump in a lake?"

Penelope looked at him and set her mouth in an amused line. "Who says that anymore?"

"I've heard my sixty-year-old father say it," Joey said with a laugh. "I guess it's an old-fashioned phrase now."

Penelope pictured Joey's father, who he looked just alike, and wondered what she'd look like in thirty years.

"Speaking of swimming," Joey interrupted her thoughts, "Let's take a dip in the pool, cool things off a little around here." He stood up and held out his hand, helping her up from her chaise.

Penelope followed him to the water, the pavement warm beneath her feet. As she eased into the pool, she looked up at the big house next door, not seeing any sign of the Popes behind the glass.

CHAPTER 14

Penelope was on her third cup of coffee by the time she got to the studio the next morning. After a day of relaxing by the pool she and Joey made dinner at home, grilling some thick tuna steaks out on the patio and eating them with fresh salads. They'd shared a bottle of wine and gone to bed early. Penelope had thought after such a relaxing day she'd sleep soundly, but she'd woken up several times, her dreams keeping her from resting peacefully. But she had to admit the pleasant time away from work had helped her face things again when she got to the studio.

Scanning the headlines that morning she learned that Isaac was still in custody but was heading to court that day for a bail hearing. The article went on to say he had a prior arrest during his time in the states, which had complicated his release. Isaac and some friends had been involved in a bar fight several months earlier at a one of the local establishments that lined the boardwalk on Salacia Beach. The arrest in the shooting had violated his probation and had caused him more legal trouble.

Penelope remembered Isaac being gone from the set unexpectedly for a few days when the scheduled scenes they were meant to shoot had been shuffled out for ones that didn't involve him. She figured that must have been around the time of the bar fight, although that obviously hadn't been common knowledge on the film set. Penelope had finished reading the article, stuffed her iPad into her bag and left for work.

Francis had gotten into the studio kitchen first and was busy taking inventory of the walk-in refrigerator.

"Morning, Boss," he said over his shoulder as she entered.

"How are you today?" Penelope asked. Francis shrugged noncommittally.

She picked up the call sheet from the table nearest the door that the production office had left for them that morning. It listed the day's location, number of cast and crew to be fed, and estimated length of day and meal break times. There were two names at the top of the talent list she didn't recognize.

"Who are these people on the call sheet?" she asked, waving the piece of paper in at Francis's back.

"Stand-ins for the two leads," Francis said. "We're headed back to the cliffs."

Penelope bit her lip and set the call sheet back down on the table. "Come on," she muttered under her breath. How were a couple of stand-ins new to the set going to get anything different from the last fifty takes on film for Chad? She shook her head and wished once again for this project, which had become like a never-ending loop of a nightmare, to finish.

"I know," Francis said. "It's a bummer we have to go back. Like, traumatizing almost."

"How was the fish this morning?" Penelope asked after a pause. She slung her messenger bag off of her shoulder and set it on the table. The apartment building most of the out of town crew had been living in during filming was right next to one of the biggest fish markets in Salacia Beach. Francis would normally stop there on the way in to pick up the best-looking catch of the day.

Francis wiped his hands on a towel and threw it over his

shoulder, then motioned for her to follow him to the walk-in. He lugged a large gray service tub and set it on the counter.

"Rainbow trout," Francis said, hooking his index finger into the mouth of one of the fish and pulling it from the shaved ice. The overhead light glimmered on the fish's silvery scales.

"They look great," Penelope said. "Good choice."

"Morning," Javier said from the doorway. There were dark circles under his eyes but his clothes were clean and crisp, and his hair was neatly combed in its close-cropped military style.

"Hi Javier," Penelope said. "Did you get some rest?"

"Some," Javier said. "Trevor's right behind me." He stepped quickly to one of the large stainless-steel sinks near the doorway and began scrubbing his hands, like a doctor preparing for surgery. Javier had told her more than once that a chef's best tool is a clean pair of hands.

"We'll run through the day's menus and assignments once we're all here," Penelope said with a glance at the clock over the door.

"Hey, Boss," Trevor said as he came through the door. "Traffic was a beast today." His chef coat was draped over one of his long muscular arms, and he wore a tight t-shirt with a faded image of Dirty Harry across the chest.

"We're heading back to the cliffs."

Trevor groaned while Javier continued to scrub his hands.

"Javier will stay behind and inventory our stock and clean out the walk-in," Penelope said. Javier looked as if he was about to protest her decision but a glance from Penelope deterred him. He appeared to relax a bit as he listened to her list out the rest of the day's assignments and instructions.

"Okay, menu ideas. Go," she said.

"I was thinking we could do a cold soup," Trevor said. "A cauliflower puree with green chili oil. Maybe a few cold soups, like gazpacho, or honeydew melon. Served with fresh baked bread."

Penelope rubbed a finger on her chin, then jotted something down in her notebook. "Pick one soup," she said. "We can make sandwiches and fillet of trout as catch of the day. It's not going to be a long day and we only have to feed a skeleton crew of forty people. Let's hope it's an easy day, anyway."

Trevor nodded. "I think we should go with gazpacho. Goes well with trout."

"Perfect," Penelope said. "Okay, let's get the truck prepped and loaded."

After they dispersed, Javier lingered behind. "I can go back to the cliffs, you know."

"I need you here," Penelope said. "Look, you're not being punished, and I'm not feeling sorry for you. It's a light day and I can better utilize the team by having you at home base, getting us ready for the final push of this show. I don't know about you but I'm ready to wrap this one."

Javier nodded tightly. "Sure, Boss. I can do that for the team."

"I know you can," Penelope said. She squeezed his bicep then turned her focus back to her notebook.

CHAPTER 15

On the way back to the cliffs, Penelope found herself studying the sandy shoulders of the two-lane highway as their truck climbed the hill. She didn't know exactly what she was looking for, maybe some kind of clue that would make sense out of what happened along this road two days ago. But all she saw was pavement and rocky sand, and scrub brush at the edges.

Pulling into the parking area just off to the right of where they'd once again be filming, Penelope studied the various vehicles that members of the crew had driven up. One of the Teamsters, the team responsible for all of the transportation on set, was setting up the mobile restrooms for the crew to use for the day, unhooking it from the back of a large SUV that he'd hauled it up there behind. He was bent over a trailer hitch, jostling the joint between a truck and trailer which appeared to be jammed.

"Hi," Penelope said, when he caught her watching him from the edge of the lot. She buttoned up her chef coat and moved a few feet closer to him. He stood up tall, the sun behind him obscuring his features in shadow. "Penelope from catering," she said when he gave her a small shrug.

"Carl from transportation," he said. "Something wrong with your truck?" he said. "I'll come over and have a look in a minute." He gave the metal bar a swift kick with his boot and the two pieces broke free. He wore a faded denim jacket and his black work gloves were molded against his large hands. Reaching down, he began cranking the winch back into place.

"I was wondering," Penelope said, raising her voice over the screeching sound of metal on metal, "were you here when—"

"When the shooting happened?" he interrupted, grunting with exertion. "Nah, I was working out of the studio that day, moving cars around the set for a cop show pilot. I don't see that one getting picked up, if you know what I mean. Kind of a farfetched concept, a cop from outer space or something."

Penelope nodded. "Yeah, I've been on a couple of shows like that."

"But I heard about what happened. Everyone's been talking about that guy getting shot. Right in the heart," he said, wiping his brow with the back of his glove. He looked down at the winch and nodded as if pleased it had finally bent to his will and was in its proper place. "Bad news travels fast in this business."

"It sure does. It was a pretty awful day."

"Probably worse for the guy who got shot than us, though, right?" Carl said.

"True," Penelope said, eyeing the vehicles parked in the lot. "I was just trying to see how that guy got in and out of here."

"What guy?" Carl asked, looking at the cars around him like someone might be hiding there still.

"The guy who had the gun. The real gun," Penelope said.

"Oh yeah," Carl said. "The guy with the gun. Prop clerk, right?"

Penelope nodded then continued to study the cars. The sun reflected off of the windshields in the lot of about thirty vehicles. Nothing looked any different from the other day, or stood out in any way.

"My buddy Jake was working here that day," the man said, surveying the lot with her, as if the answer to her question was hiding behind one of them. Giving up the search, he leaned against the side of the SUV and crossed his arms in front of him. "He said he saw the whole thing go down, you know, the shooting."

"Is your friend here today?" Penelope asked.

"Nah, he got the union to get him pulled out of this mess. Mental anguish, he claimed to them. I'm the lucky one they put in his place," he said with a flat expression on his face. "I don't have any anguish. Not yet, anyway."

"Which one is Jake? What does he look like?" Penelope asked.

"I don't know," Carl said. "Tall, I guess, brown hair. Why are you asking about what he looks like?"

"I'm just trying to picture him," Penelope said evasively. "We have a lot of people in and out of here and, you know, I like to remember everyone. Makes it faster when they order breakfast if I recognize them."

He looked at her skeptically, like she was a used car salesman. "Jake didn't shoot Sebastian, if that's what you're getting at."

Penelope's cheeks reddened and she cleared her throat. "I wasn't saying—"

"He's in LA working on a set today. Pretty sure he wouldn't be if he was a stone-cold killer."

It was Penelope's turn to look skeptical. "Did Jake tell you anything about the property handler?"

"Nah," Carl said with a sigh. He stood up straight and took a few steps away from her, apparently finished with their conversation. "Anyway, the cops questioned everyone so...you're the caterer, right?"

"Yeah," Penelope said. "I'm just having a hard time remembering. I was right there when it happened and..."

"You're the one who jumped over the table and gave Sebastian mouth to mouth," Carl said. "Jake told me, you jumped in and tried to save him."

"Well," Penelope said. "Not exactly, but yeah." Penelope had only pressed on Sebastian's gunshot wound. She wondered if this Jake person had actually been there at all, or had only heard about what happened.

"That was good of you," Carl said. He pulled off one of his gloves and tucked it under his arm. His face was round and soft, which didn't match the lean angular frame of his body. "I can ask Jake if he saw the guy with the gun next time I see him."

"Don't worry about it," Penelope said with a wave of her hand, already concerned she'd tipped her hand too much to this virtual stranger. "I'm sure the police have asked him already. I should get back to work."

"Yeah. It will all get figured out," Carl said. "You can't hide for long in this town."

Penelope thought about her favorite podcast and all of the cold cases from around the state she'd been learning about, but decided to just agree with Carl and head back to her truck to mull things over on her own.

On her way back, she paused when she got to the actor's trailers. They were parked around the perimeter, in between the lot and the parking area. The trailer Sebastian had been using was parked in its usual spot, and Penelope went to the door, looking over her shoulder before reaching up to pull it open.

The door opened out suddenly and Penelope stepped back as one of the PAs emerged. He was talking to someone in the trailer, his head turned away from Penelope. She watched him finish up what he was saying and step out onto the metal landing of the staircase and begin to close the door.

"Oh," he said when he saw her standing there. "Did you

need to talk to him too?"

"Yes," Penelope said as he trotted down the stairs. "Just real quick."

The PA shrugged and hurried away, leaving the door open behind him. Penelope trotted up the steps and ducked inside after a quick knock on the door.

"Sorry to bother you," Penelope said.

The stand-in was inside, looking at himself in a full-length mirror next to the makeup table. "No bother, come on in."

"I just wanted to see if we could bring you anything before you get started today," Penelope said. "A coffee, juice, or whatever?"

The young man turned, and Penelope studied his face. He didn't look anything like Sebastian, but he was wearing the same suit Sebastian had worn in the scene. The one he was wearing when he died. "That's nice of you," he said in a deep voice. He turned back to the mirror and adjusted his collar. "A coffee would be wonderful."

"Sure," Penelope said. "I'll have one of the guys bring it." She looked around the space at the different countertops and cabinets. It appeared that Sebastian's belongings had been cleared out. "How do you take it?"

"Sorry?" he asked, looking at her in the mirror.

"Your coffee," Penelope said. "What do you like in it?" She eased open a cabinet next to her and peered inside.

"Black, straight up," he said. "Looking for something?"

"Yes," Penelope said. "We stock the trailers with snacks and things, so I was just checking."

"Feel free," he said. "I'm only here today, so you don't have to go to any trouble on my account."

"Oh," Penelope said, with some relief at the possibility of not returning to the cliffs ever again. She opened a few more cabinets, then slid out a drawer in the kitchen.

"The police were all over this wagon after the accident," the young actor said. "I don't think they left anything behind." He apparently wasn't buying her catering excuse for snooping through Sebastian's space.

"I see," she said, deflating.

"But I found this," he said, picking up an envelope from the makeup counter and turning around to face her again. "They missed it somehow. Probably because it was taped under the table here."

"What is it?" Penelope asked.

"Fan mail," he said with a shrug. "I was going to bring it out with me, hand it over to Chad so he could get it to...whoever is collecting the guys personal belongings."

"I'll take it," Penelope said. "Get it to Chad for you."

He handed it to her with another shrug. "It's just some letters, not sure why it was where it was, but I've learned to not be surprised by anything people do anymore."

Penelope fingered open the envelope and looked inside. There were several handwritten letters inside. "I know what you mean," she mumbled.

"I'll be out in a few minutes, just going to freshen up. Thanks for the coffee." As he headed toward the bathroom, she took her leave, tucking the envelope into her coat pocket as she headed back to her truck.

CHAPTER 16

A few hours later after Penelope sent her team home, she sat down to do her paperwork in her office at the studio after stripping off her apron and chef coat and draping them across the back of her chair. Feeling the outline of the envelope still in her pocket, she pulled it out and placed it on her desk. She'd forgotten to give it to Chad earlier and wrote herself a note to hand it to him the next time she saw him.

"We've got the final scenes to finish and that's it," Chad said in a flat tone when she checked in with him on the set. "I've been let go, but I have to finish principal filming or they'll say I didn't fulfill my contract. Have you ever been fired, and then asked to keep working?"

"No," Penelope said.

"They're going to bring in someone else to do post production, and I'm not getting the director credit on the movie as punishment for my involvement," Chad said.

"Wow," Penelope said. "I'm sorry to hear that."

Chad's bony shoulders shrugged under his baggy t-shirt. "Whatever. Calvin blames me for running a disorganized set. And for Sebastian dying on a Pope Productions film."

"Did you know about anyone who might have wanted to hurt Sebastian?" Penelope asked.

Chad shook his head. "I mean, the guy was difficult. I'm sure I'm not the only person he's rubbed the wrong way over the years. But I didn't have anything to do with this."

Penelope watched him walk back to his chair. None of the enthusiasm he'd had on his first day of filming remained. It had all melted away over the past several weeks.

A much more subdued Chad had the stand-ins run through the scene half a dozen times before calling it a day. Penelope was relieved they were officially done, and wouldn't be returning to that particular location again, and that Chad had decided he had what he needed to hand over to post-production on the movie, so filming was essentially wrapped. They were all told to be on call for a few more days in the event they needed to make up any scenes, but very soon they could all say goodbye to *Severed Lives*.

Penelope filled out the payroll reports for her team and walked them down to production, which was past the conference room area and executive offices. Tapping on the door first, then easing it open, Penelope slid her paperwork into the inbox sitting on the administrative assistant's desk.

"Just turning in today's hours," Penelope said as Bernice looked up at her from her computer screen. She'd been studying something intently when Penelope entered.

"Done for the day?" she asked, eyeing the envelope Penelope had set down. Penelope knew from experience that Bernice didn't respond well if the payroll reports were incomplete, and the paperwork had to be submitted in a particular order or she'd send it back to be completed again. She looked at the envelope with suspicion, like instead of timesheets there was an intricate puzzle inside she was being asked to work out.

"I remembered to total all of the hours up this time," Penelope said, heading off her question.

Bernice lifted her eyebrows and returned Penelope's smile.

"Thank you. I appreciate that."

Bernice Mabley's office was neat and compact, with a single framed photo on her desk of her holding her arms in the shape of a "V" in front of a huge wave. Next to it was her laptop and three tidy stacks of paper. Bernice apparently didn't believe in unnecessary clutter or knickknacks on her desk, or on the one doublewide filing cabinet beneath the picture window that overlooked the Pacific behind her. In the far corner next to the window was a door that led to Scarlett's executive suite. Bernice acted as Scarlett's assistant but also kept all of Pope Productions' projects on schedule and made sure the bills and payroll were processed too. Penelope had gotten to know her over the past months because she also coordinated all of the department head meetings. Bernice managed all of this from the sleek laptop in front of her, and without a hair out of place. She was efficiency personified.

"I think maybe we're done filming all together. Thank goodness," Penelope said.

"You were on *Severed Lives* the whole time, right?" Bernice asked, her eyes flicking back to her screen. Penelope felt like she knew the answer to her question, but it was her way of making conversation.

"For three months," Penelope said. "Hey, by any chance did the police ask for the call sheets for the other day, you know—"

"The day of the incident?" Bernice responded crisply. She brushed some nonexistent dust from her desk. "Yes, we made copies of everything for them to take, for use in the investigation."

"Were there any discrepancies with the prop department that you remember?" Penelope asked.

"No...well, yes," she said, drawing the word out. "The names matched up to known employees of Pope Productions, although the property assistant on your set was assigned to two places at once." She shook her head slightly, annoyed by the blatant discrepancy.

"What do you mean, two places at once?" Penelope said.

"I probably shouldn't say, it being an active police investigation," Bernice hedged. Then she leaned forward like she wanted to give her opinion quietly. "There are privacy rules. Corporate ones, union, you know." There was a glint in her eye when she met Penelope's gaze, as if she thought there could be exceptions to those rules.

"I was on that set," Penelope said. "And I'm one of the department supervisors on the call sheets, so...I should probably know if someone reported to our set and ate the company-purchased food without authorization."

"Oh well, that makes sense," Bernice said, visibly relieved she'd been released from the chains of the Pope Production's privacy policy. Her thin fingers flitted from her blouse's collar to her chin, and she lowered her voice after a glance at Scarlett's office door behind her. "Somehow the same person's name showed up on a set in downtown Salacia Beach, and also up on the cliff location, with not enough time in between to get to both places."

"Wow," Penelope said. "Someone messed up then, right?"

Bernice nodded and set her mouth in a grim line.

"Who was it?" Penelope asked.

"Who?" Bernice asked. She appeared alarmed, like she'd forgotten to relay some important piece of information.

"The prop guy," Penelope said. "What's his name?"

"Bill Smith."

"Smith?" Penelope asked, deflating.

Bernice shrugged slightly and nodded. "He's a day player, not an employee, so we pay him a per diem whenever he picks up work on one of our productions. His file checks out," she added a bit defensively. "The police confirmed that's his actual name, and that he wasn't at the cliffs that day, and was working on another project of ours down on Salacia Beach. So...that's what they know right now."

"How did his name get onto two call sheets?" Penelope asked.

"Someone logged in and assigned him to the cliffs location," Bernice said. "But the real Bill Smith had been working on the beach shoot for a couple of weeks, and went where he usually went. He didn't know anything about the discrepancy."

"So someone with access to the scheduling program filled in a prop handler spot with Bill's name..." Penelope said.

"Right," Bernice said with a nod. They heard a cough behind Scarlett's door and Bernice put a finger to her lips and widened her eyes.

Penelope nodded and lowered her voice. "So this 'Bill,'" she hooked her fingers into air quotes, "signed in with the location manager on my set."

"I guess so," Bernice said with a slight shake of her head.

"Does that kind of thing happen a lot? You know, clerical...errors?" Penelope said, grimacing as if she was talking about a cancer diagnosis as opposed to a paperwork mishap.

"I mean, mistakes happen," Bernice said, straightening a pen on her desk to line up with her blotter. "Not by me. But they happen."

"But this time it wasn't a mistake. Someone did this on purpose," Penelope said. "Someone adds Bill to the call sheet, and the location manager would just take it for granted that the right person was on the correct set. It's not like we show our IDs when we get there."

"No, not always. Maybe on the first day, but not at the end," she said. "It would've been the same crew for the most part for weeks. Although after this...mistake, and the event that happened because of it...Mr. Pope might be tightening up their procedures."

Penelope had always associated the word "event" with something pleasant, like a wedding or graduation, not something that resulted in death. "I suppose someone could use a fake ID too, as long as the name on it matched up to the call sheet."

"We have name badges on lanyards that we give to visitors to the set," Bernice said. "You know, guests, or screenwriters, or different investors who come through town but aren't regularly here. But we don't require our contracted employees to wear anything while they're working. Again, I'm sure that will change from now on."

"Still, someone could fake one of those probably. My friend in school had a driver's license that wasn't hers, but it had her picture on it."

"Like we used to use to get into bars," Bernice said with a knowing grin. Penelope tried to picture prim and proper Bernice throwing back a shot in some bar and couldn't quite manage it.

"So, basically, it's pretty easy to crash a movie set," Penelope asked.

"Afraid so," Bernice said. "Some of our productions have three or four hundred people working on location...it's up to the supervisors for each department, lighting, sound, transportation, property, to keep track of their teams."

"And if they don't..." Penelope said.

"Things can happen," she said. "There was a guy not too long ago who said he was a tutor. He was hired to fulfill the state's educational requirements on set for the kids. Turns out he wasn't who he said he was, he wasn't even a teacher at all."

"Oh wow," Penelope said. "When did he work here?"

"He didn't," Bernice said. "The guy made his way onto a set my brother Paul was working on. Paul's a stunt man, he works on shows and movies all over the state, mostly out of LA. Anyway, this tutor guy got caught. It was in all the papers."

"I missed that story," Penelope said.

"He duped a lot of people, conned his way onto half a dozen movie sets with a phony résumé and fake references."

"Did he...hurt any of the kids?" Penelope asked, her stomach dropping at the thought.

"Nothing was reported by any of the children or the parents, thank God," Bernice said. "The guy said he just needed the work and was a good teacher."

"Then why not get certified and do it the way you're supposed to?" Penelope asked. She was suddenly just as passionate about rules and order as Bernice was.

"Who knows why people do things," Bernice said. "But he can think about it now that he's banned from ever working in the industry again."

"Someone like that would probably think of a way to do it again," Penelope mused. "Use another name, or move somewhere else to try it again."

"I hope not," Bernice said. "I do know things will change from now on around here. There will be more accountability, more security put in place. We will have to."

"That's probably for the best," Penelope said.

"Too bad it takes a tragedy for people to act," Bernice said with a slow shake of her head. Another cough came from behind Scarlett's door. "And sometimes that's not even enough," she added in a whisper.

*   *   *

Back at her desk, Penelope stared at the envelope containing Sebastian's fan mail for a second, then opened the browser on her computer and Googled Sebastian's name. The screen filled with results about his death, articles written from around the world, the most recent updated within the last hour. They all rehashed the same basic information, the movie set shooting, Isaac Lee's connection, brief bios of Sebastian's life and career. Rubbing her chin with her finger she read through the headlines quickly, then typed Brogan Pope after his name in the search bar.

Nothing came from that search except a few articles about Sebastian's work with Pope Productions. She didn't know what Brogan's name had been before she'd married Calvin, and her name didn't show up on a quick search of popular Australian soap operas. She could have sworn Calvin told her Brogan and Sebastian had worked together before, but maybe Brogan's role on the show hadn't been lengthy enough to be notable. Penelope scanned through a few more articles, then sat back and sighed. Picking up the envelope, she pulled out the letters, opening the first one and reading through the scrawled words.

There were five letters in total, all of them appearing to be from fans, complimenting Sebastian on his work on favorite television shows or films. One was a little on the racy side, and Penelope's cheeks blushed as she read one woman's private thoughts about what she and Sebastian could've meant to each other. None of the names of the letter writers meant anything to Penelope, and none of them stood out as threatening or out of the ordinary, apart from being quite passionate feelings on the part of Sebastian's fans. She folded them back up and went to tuck them back into the envelope when she noticed a small photograph tucked into the bottom of it. Tipping it over she shook it slightly until it slid out. A small black and white photo, like the ones from those booths at carnivals or on the boardwalk had been torn in half. A girl's face stared up at her from her desk from the remaining half.

Penelope picked up the picture carefully and studied the young woman, who looked to be no older than sixteen or so in the picture. She hoped it wasn't the same person who had written the explicit letter to Sebastian, only because she looked too young and innocent to have those kinds of adult thoughts. Someone had written on the back of the photo, but the words had been cut in half too. What remained were a jumble of letters that made no sense, but that Penelope figured could be the first part of a name. She looked in the envelope to see if the other half was still inside, but it was empty.

After another long look at the girl, Penelope tucked the picture and letters back into the envelope and tucked it into the top drawer of her desk, then slid it closed.

A half hour later Penelope shut off the lights in the studio kitchen and slung her bag over her shoulder. As she stepped out into the late afternoon heat, she paused just outside the front doors of the studio and watched a van full of crew members pull into the lot, wondering what location they were returning from. As the men piled out of the car, she noticed they were all dressed in similar clothes, all of them in jeans and t-shirts, all of them wearing boots. As they headed toward her, she studied their faces, trying to pick out anything familiar about any of them, and match them up to the man she'd seen two days ago. As the faces passed, they all began to blend together in her mind.

"Safe home," one of them said in a gravelly voice as he

passed, yanking open the glass door and stepping inside.

"Yep," Penelope said. After they'd all gone inside, Penelope straightened the strap over her shoulder and headed out to the parking lot. She couldn't wait to get home.

CHAPTER 17

Penelope felt the pressure on her chest before her eyes opened. In her dream Sebastian was pressing on her sternum while Bernice looked on, a martini glass in one hand and a photograph of a faceless man in the other. Penelope tried to call out, to tell him he was pressing too hard, but it was like she was speaking through a pane of glass, and they were on the other side, unable to hear anything she said.

Penelope began to suffocate from the pressure, both from the crushing feeling on her chest and from trying to picture the man's face. While she concentrated on that, she'd forgotten how to pull air in and out of her lungs. She tried to twist onto her side and out from under Sebastian, but he held her firmly, leaving her gasping for air.

"Who did this?" he said from behind the glass, his words barely seeping through. He looked like he was lip synching, the words she heard not matching up with the movements of his mouth.

Penelope's eyes flew open and she sputtered a cough, pulling in a ragged breath. A pair of sleek green eyes stared into hers and she froze as she listened to the blood rush through her ears. Joey snored quietly beside her, asleep on his side turned away from her toward the open window.

Mirabella was perched on Penelope's chest, gazing down at her.

"What are you doing in here?" Penelope whispered hoarsely. The room was dark, the moon hidden behind a cloudy sky, the sun still hours away from peeking through the drapes that wafted in the slight breeze.

The cat's purrs vibrated Penelope's chest.

Penelope eased into a seated position and nudged Mirabella onto her lap, still disoriented from her dream. The longing for air, the feeling of being smothered, and seeing Sebastian's face had rattled her.

She turned on the bedside lamp and then looked back at the cat. Joey groaned and adjusted his pillow. It was four in the morning, but for him it would feel more like one o'clock. He was still operating on east coast time.

"What happened? What's on you?" Penelope gently touched a finger to Mirabella's head, which was matted down and wet looking. She held her finger closer to her face then jerked it away when she realized it was blood.

"Joey," Penelope said, nudging him with her other hand. "Wake up!"

Mirabella meowed at Penelope, like she was trying to communicate something.

"What happened?" Joey said groggily, sitting up in the bed and looking at the cat in Penelope's lap. "I thought you said you didn't have a cat."

"What?"

Joey rubbed his eyes and yawned. "Bad joke, sorry. How did the cat get in here?"

"I guess she came in through the balcony," Penelope said.

"I told you to close it," Joey said. "It's not safe."

"We're on the second floor," Penelope said defensively. "No one is scaling the walls out there. And the ocean air is nice."

Joey looked at the cat then up at Penelope. "She got in here, so there's a way in. And it's not safe."

Penelope looked down at Mirabella and let his comment go. He was right, and she never left the door cracked open when he wasn't there. But Chardonnay Court was so deserted most of the time, it was just her and the Popes. Mirabella stared at her as she reached out her finger to show to Joey.

"Where did the blood come from?" he asked, suddenly alert. Joey threw the covers back from his legs and went to the window.

"Maybe she killed a mouse or something," Penelope said.

"And got blood all over her head?" Joey said doubtfully.

"Well, what else could it be from? She's not injured, I don't think," Penelope said. "Is there anyone out there down by the pool?"

Joey shook his head as he craned his neck to get a better view of the patio below. "There's a bloody paw print on the balcony out here. She must have climbed up the trellis."

"She's never done that before," Penelope said.

Joey returned to his side of the bed, picking up his jeans from the floor on his way and pulling them on. "I'm going downstairs to check it out."

"Check what out?" Penelope said.

"Penny," Joey said, "your neighbor's cat turns up in your bed and has blood on her, enough to trail across your balcony. How do you think that happened?"

Penelope's heart sank. "Maybe Mirabella ran into a coyote, like you said."

"Maybe, but I don't think so, Penny."

"Do think someone next door could be hurt?" Her mind flashed back to the heated argument they'd overheard the day before between the Popes.

"I'm going to check it out," Joey said.

"Let's call the police," Penelope countered.

"Look," Joey said, pulling on his shirt. He slid open the drawer of the nightstand and retrieved his gun, tucking it in his waistband at the small of his back. "I'm going to see if everything is okay next door. If it isn't, we'll call the police. Okay?"

"I'm coming with you," Penelope said. She eased Mirabella off of her lap and got out of the bed, heading for the easy chair in the corner where she'd tossed her jeans and a sweatshirt before climbing into bed.

"No, you wait here," Joey said.

"Not a chance," Penelope said, dismissing any further argument.

Joey sighed. "Okay, but you stay way back while I look. I don't want you getting hurt. It's probably nothing. Maybe she killed a rat or something like you said."

Penelope stepped into the bathroom to scrub the blood from her hand, watching the pink stained swirl down the drain. "Gross," she said over the running water.

"Let's go," Joey said after she'd finished.

Mirabella watched them leave, not moving from the warmth of the bed.

CHAPTER 18

At first glance, everything seemed normal at the Pope's house. The front door was closed, and only a soft orange glow filtered through the windows. Penelope followed closely behind Joey, even though he kept urging her to keep back as they approached the house from the sidewalk. The garage door was closed, and there were no unfamiliar vehicles in the cul-de-sac. The sounds of the waves crashing behind the house sounded louder than usual, amplified by the still evening air.

As they climbed the porch steps, they could see that the front door wasn't closed and was shifting back and forth slightly with the ocean breeze.

Joey tented his fingers and pushed on the door, easing it open. He pulled his gun from the small of his back with one hand and put his finger to his lips with the other, motioning for Penelope to wait on the porch. She reluctantly agreed and watched him take a step over the threshold.

After what seemed like five minutes, she heard Joey's voice from the other side of the door. "Calvin?" He called out. "Brogan? Are you home?"

Penelope's stomach tightened and an overwhelming impulse to leave right then overcame her. She thought about the blood she washed from her hand and knew she didn't want to be the one to discover whatever had happened to cause someone to bleed. She fought the urge to go back to her bungalow, lock the doors, and pull the covers over her head.

A moan floated down from somewhere on the upper level. Penelope heard Joey's footsteps retreat to the back of the house. Unable to wait any longer, she stepped inside and headed toward the kitchen. There were clothes strewn across the hallway floor, brightly colored dresses and scarves, like a suitcase had broken open and no one had stopped to pick up the spilled contents.

Joey appeared at the top of the spiral glass stairway. A bloody handprint was streaked across the bluish glass halfway down. Penelope's heart started beating loudly as she stared at it, unable to pull her eyes away.

"Penny. Call 911," Joey said calmly. "Have them send an ambulance."

Penelope fumbled her phone out of her back pocket and dialed emergency, then looked back up at the bloody handprint. An operator picked up after the first ring.

"Ambulance," Joey repeated.

Penelope relayed the information to the operator, feeling the thud of her heartbeat at the back of her throat. Joey stepped away from the top of the stairs and ducked back into the master suite. She hung up and her eyes fell to the sliding glass doors that led out to the Popes' back yard, walking toward it on shaky legs. A piece of broken glass crunched under her shoe and she paused, looking down at the remnants of a wine glass that had been smashed into a hundred pieces, a pool of burgundy liquid flung out around it.

The glass door was open, the gauzy coral colored curtain billowing out around it. Shivering, Penelope stood next to the dining room table and leaned on it for support for a second before getting closer to look outside.

"Don't touch anything," Joey called down. He had appeared again at the top of the stairway.

Penelope jumped and put a hand to her chest. "I won't. I stepped on some glass, though." She looked down. Near her feet was more of the shattered goblet. "Joey, what happened?"

"Stay put," Joey said. The sound of sirens approaching tightened the grip Penelope felt in her chest. Joey started up the stairs slowly, being careful not to step on any evidence or touch the railings.

Penelope looked at the floor. Someone had flung a wine glass, or maybe it had fallen off the table during a struggle. It was the same type of glass Penelope had drunk from the other night. Maybe even the same glass. The dining table was set for two, and remnants of a partially eaten meal had begun to dry out and harden onto the plates. They'd had salmon with sweet potatoes and wilted spinach, but had stopped eating halfway through. Was it some kind of home invasion in the middle of dinner?

There was another blood smear on the edge of the island. Penelope stepped away from it as she heard a siren stop right outside the front door. Joey met her at the counter and pulled her stiffly toward him, wrapping his arm gruffly around her shoulders.

"It's going to be okay," he said unconvincingly.

"Is it Brogan?" Penelope said, her voice cracking. "Is she hurt up there?"

Two paramedics pushed through the front door and paused in the front hall. Joey let go of Penelope and headed toward them.

"Unconscious male, mid-sixties with wrist lacerations, facial cuts and bruises, a scalp injury upstairs in the master bath. There's a lot of blood," Joey said.

The paramedics stepped quickly up the front stairway.

"What about Brogan?" Penelope asked. "Is she hurt too?"

"She's not here, from what I can tell," Joey said. "I checked all the rooms upstairs in case she was hurt and needed help. She might be out on the grounds...I don't know. I didn't want to contaminate the scene any more than we already have."

He stepped gingerly over to the sliding glass door and eyed the handprint, then slipped through the opening onto the back patio, being careful not to brush the edges of the doorframe. Penelope followed, trying to step where he had.

"Watch it," Joey said, pointing at the wooden deck beneath their feet. What looked like droplets of blood led from the doorway to the railing.

"Police," a voice boomed from inside. "Anyone here?"

Joey pulled out his wallet and flipped it open to reveal his identification. "Out here on the porch," he said.

"You the one who called?" A uniformed police officer peered through the doorway.

"I did," Penelope said.

"You live here?" he asked, stepping outside. He trained his eyes across them and then to the surrounding deck.

"No, we live next door," Penelope said.

Joey showed the officer his New Jersey State Homicide ID and badge, then tucked his wallet back in his pocket.

"You live next door in New Jersey?" he asked.

"Well, I live next door," Penelope said, tripping over her words. "He's visiting but staying with me too."

"What brings you over here in the middle of the night?" he asked, relaxing slightly. "Your party got out of control?"

"No," Penelope said quickly. "My friends, well, my employer and his wife, we've become friendly so I'm here sometimes but..." Penelope sputtered.

Joey put a reassuring hand on the small of her back. "Slow down," he mumbled.

"I know the Popes," Penelope said after a deep breath. "I've been living next door for a few months. I also work out of Pope Productions, and I've been over for dinner several times."

"Okay," the officer said, still appearing unsure she was telling him the whole story. "And you, what, stop over to visit in the middle of the night sometimes?" The bridge of his nose was sunburned, and Penelope kept her eyes there, wondering if he'd been out of the golf course earlier, and wishing he'd remembered his sunscreen or hat before he left the house.

"Their cat climbed through our bedroom window and woke us up," Joey said, shaking her from her thoughts. "The cat had blood on her. We were concerned for the safety of the residents here and came to check on them. The front door was open, and I did a welfare check after I noticed blood on the premises, and signs of a struggle."

The officer nodded, seeming to approve of Joey's concise and professional accounting of events. "Okay. Come back inside and have a seat while I call for a detective. You know the drill, I'm sure."

Joey nodded. "Whatever you need, Officer."

Penelope and Joey followed him inside and took a seat in the seating area on the other side of the fireplace.

"Where is Brogan?" Penelope asked again after he'd stepped away to make a call.

Joey eyed the spilled wine on the floor and the abandoned meal on the table, settling on the bloody handprint on the door. "It's hard to say exactly. There was some kind of altercation or struggle in here, that's for sure."

"Maybe they had an argument over dinner," Penelope said. The odor of fish that had been out in the open too long wafted through the air.

"Or someone interrupted their dinner," Joey said. "Remember, we heard them making up after the last argument. Some couples fight as a part of their...I don't know, dynamic, I guess."

"But if there was someone else here that did this...what happened to Brogan?" Penelope felt her heart rate begin to speed up. "What if she's been kidnapped, Joey?"

"Let's not get ahead of ourselves," Joey said. "They'll know more if they get a forensics team here."

"Right," Penelope said.

"Unless it was a fight gone bad between a husband and wife," Joey said. "In that case they'll call it a domestic and Calvin and Brogan might have charges pressed against one of both of them."

"Oh no," Penelope said. "I don't want for them to have been attacked, of course, but I don't want to think of them hurting each other either."

Joey shrugged and put his arm around her shoulders. Penelope leaned into him.

"Did Calvin try to kill himself?" she whispered, leaning forward to see where the officer had gone. "I heard you mention he had injuries on his wrists."

Joey shrugged. "It's possible."

"Maybe Brogan just had enough and said she was leaving. You heard them yesterday," Penelope continued in her whisper. "What if they were fighting again and this time things got physical? And Brogan left, causing Calvin to...?"

Joey looked at her, his eyebrows raised. "End it all? I mean, you know Calvin better than me, but he doesn't strike me as the kind of guy who goes to pieces over a breakup."

"True," Penelope said. "But we don't really know for sure."

"That's why the police are involved. They'll figure it out."

"Someone should be looking for Brogan," Penelope said, leaning against him harder. A wave of exhaustion fell over her at the same time Joey stifled a yawn. "I want to go home."

"We have to wait, unfortunately," Joey said. "Now I know how it feels when I hold witnesses at a scene."

Penelope closed her eyes and pictured her bed next door, hoping they could get back to sleep soon.

Detectives Zahn and Adalbert came down the hallway just as the paramedics hefted the still unconscious Calvin down the front stairs on a stretcher. They paused to look at him and ask a few questions before proceeding to the sitting room where Penelope and Joey waited. Calvin's head and half of his face was wrapped in a white bandage, and his wrists had thick gauze wrapped around them. An oxygen mask had been strapped over his mouth and nose, and a portable monitor beeped between his splayed legs.

"Penelope Sutherland," Adalbert said, "we meet again."

"Twice in one week," Zahn said, eyeing her up and down.

"Detectives," Penelope said. "This is Joseph Baglioni."

"New Jersey Homicide," Joey said with a nod.

"Freelancing on the West Coast?" Detective Zahn said, still sizing up the two of them. Penelope looked down at yesterday's jeans and wrinkled t-shirt she'd pulled on before heading next door. She knew she looked disheveled, but she figured considering the circumstances she was presentable and undeserving of the intense scrutiny Zahn was giving her clothes.

"No freelancing," Joey said. "Just out here for vacation. My department sent an email to local PD before I arrived as a courtesy."

A small sigh escaped Zahn before she set her mouth in a tight line.

"The responding officer tells us you live next door, came to check on things over here and discovered a crime scene. That right?" Adalbert asked. He pulled a pad from his pocket and jotted something down.

"That's correct," Penelope said. "I think you should be out looking for Calvin's wife, Brogan."

"You haven't seen her tonight?" Adalbert asked, still jotting notes.

Penelope rubbed her chin with her finger and watched him write on the pad. "No. I saw her briefly yesterday when she came to get her cat."

"Why should we be looking for her? Are you concerned for her safety?" Zahn asked.

"Of course I'm concerned for her safety. Look at this place," Penelope said.

Zahn nodded. "Could be they had an argument, she takes off and the old man can't deal with it, tries to off himself."

"Or, someone came in here and attacked them both while they were having dinner," Joey offered. "And whoever that is has taken her."

"Also a possibility," Adalbert said.

"Maybe they came in from the back yard. Then disappeared back over the railing."

"Wait here," Zahn said. She stepped carefully, avoiding the shattered glass, to the door and outside, shimmying sideways like Joey had to avoid brushing her clothes against the edges.

"When was the last time you saw your neighbors?" Detective Adalbert asked.

"I was over for dinner a few nights ago," Penelope said. "The next day we heard them both outside. They were arguing." She threw a guilty look at Joey, like she'd divulged a secret she shouldn't have.

"Outside where?" he asked.

"From my side of the wall over there. We were sitting by the pool," Penelope pointed toward the adobe wall and her house just beyond.

Perking up and making another note, Adalbert said, "What were they arguing about?"

"They were arguing about the shooting, I think," Penelope said. "The one on the set. Brogan was accusing Calvin of only caring about money."

"Money. The number one topic for marital arguments," Adalbert said, thumbing his wedding ring.

"It sounded like they made up at the end, though," Joey said. "They went back inside and we didn't hear anything else the rest of the day."

"Adalbert," Detective Zahn said from the doorway. "A moment?"

"Excuse me," he said, then stepped briskly toward his partner. "Have a seat, we might have some more questions."

Joey stifled a yawn as they sat back down on the sofa in front of the fireplace. "It's always nice to get away from it all on vacation, you know?"

Penelope laughed weakly. "I'm so sorry this happened." She leaned against his shoulder and closed her eyes, feeling like she could fall asleep and stay in that spot until morning.

CHAPTER 19

Penelope watched one of the forensic techs place Mirabella into a cat carrier and slip it into the back of one of the crime scene unit's vans. The CSU team had arrived just as Detective Adalbert was escorting Penelope and Joey back to her house to retrieve the cat.

Official vehicles lined the cul-de-sac, and people in a variety of uniforms went in and out of the Popes' house, carrying empty bags inside and then full ones out. Joey brought two mugs of coffee out onto the front porch and handed Penelope one of them. The sun had just begun to rise and it lit the sky in shades of orange and pink.

"It's all clear now," the forensic tech said as she emerged from Penelope's house. "I took a few samples from your bedspread, photographed the trellis outside. Thanks for your patience while we collected the blood. I know you must be tired."

"It's okay," Penelope said. Her eyes felt sandy at the edges and she wondered how long she'd be able to stay awake before crashing into a nap. She blew on the hot coffee and took a small sip. "Where are you taking the cat?"

"To the crime lab to collect blood samples, then Animal Control will hold her until the owner can claim her."

"Oh, well I can take care of her," Penelope glanced at the house next door. "Until things get figured out."

The tech shrugged. "That's fine with the city. You just have to get the okay from the owners, fill out the paperwork, and claim the animal."

Joey glanced at her with raised eyebrows as the tech headed down the steps. "I asked you if you had a cat now..." he teased.

"Stop," Penelope said. "I just don't like to think about her being held in a cage somewhere," Penelope said. "She's going to be scared, I think."

"You're such a softy," Joey said with a smile. "One of the reasons I love you." He sat down on a wicker chair next to the front window and cradled his coffee mug in his hand.

Penelope sat next to him in the matching chair and sighed. "How do things like this happen?"

"Things like what?" Joey asked.

Penelope tilted her head toward the Popes' house.

"Domestic violence, if that's what this is, is very common, unfortunately. One in three women and one in four men will experience it in their lives, statistically speaking."

"That many?" Penelope asked.

"Unfortunately it's true," Joey said. "We heard them arguing. Obviously, every marriage has moments that aren't perfect. Sometimes we don't know how bad things are, looking in from the outside."

"I know," Penelope said. "But I've gotten to know Calvin and Brogan...I can't picture them being violent with each other. Or Calvin trying to take his own life. He's seems so carefree and confident."

"A confident older man married to a much younger woman," Joey reminded her. "Maybe there was tension because of the age difference."

"Poor Scarlett," Penelope said. "Do you think I should call her?"

"Sure," Joey said. "But give her some time. She'll be at the hospital with her father probably. Do you know where her mother is, her birth mother, I mean?"

"I don't," Penelope said. "I've never heard Calvin or Scarlett mention her."

"Hopefully, whoever she is, can help Scarlett deal with things," Joey said.

They watched until the last official vehicle had left then went inside. Another beautiful morning was underway, but it wasn't quite enough to distract Penelope from flashing back to the images of the chaos they'd found next door.

"I'm going to call the hospital," Penelope said. She put her phone on speaker and laid it on the countertop while Joey refreshed their coffee. Listening through the automated prompts she said "Calvin Pope" when asked to state a patient's name.

A metallic noise clicked on the phone and then an actual person's voice. "Hello, thanks for calling Salacia Beach Medical Center. Our records show we have a patient here by that name, but he's not allowed any calls or visitors at the moment," the receptionist at the hospital chirped over the phone.

"Oh," Penelope said. "Can you tell me if he's okay?"

"I can only tell you he's in stable condition," the woman said, "and he's under observation."

"Okay, thank you." Penelope hung up and looked at Joey. "It sounds like he's going to be okay. They're keeping him under observation."

"That's what I figured would happen," Joey said. "Doctors can place you on a psychiatric hold if they think you're a danger to yourself or others."

"How long does that last usually?" Penelope asked.

"Most of the time it's seventy-two hours," Joey said.

"Because of the injuries to his wrists, do you think?"

"That would be my guess."

Penelope sat at the kitchen island, thinking. Her phone buzzed and she looked at the screen. "I just can't see him doing that."

"But how well do you know Calvin, Penny?" Joey asked. "You've known him for a short amount of time, mostly working together. We can't always tell when someone is troubled until it's too late."

"You're right," Penelope said. "I know you are." Her phone vibrated on the counter and the screen lit up. Picking it up to read the text message, Penelope groaned and put her other hand over her eyes.

"What's up?"

"The studio just messaged to report in tomorrow morning," she said. "We have more reshoots on *Severed Lives*. Also known as 'the movie that wouldn't die.'"

"I'm sorry," Joey said. "But at least we have today together. Let's make the most of it. After a nap."

CHAPTER 20

"Javier," Penelope said as she slid her knife through the white underbelly of a rainbow trout the next morning. "Have you ever had a cat?"

"No," Javier said. "I mean, there were cats in the neighborhood, but they kind of belonged to everybody."

"Alley cats?" Penelope asked.

The usually serious Javier appeared to be in a jovial mood this morning.

"Yeah, I grew up in Broadway-Manchester," Javier said. "South of downtown LA."

"So you've never taken care of one, like in your house," Penelope said. She kept her eyes on the fish as she pulled out its guts and began to fillet the flesh into perfectly even four-ounce portions. Luckily, they were not headed to the cliffs again that day. They were going to one of the local beaches to reshoot a scene from several weeks before with a much smaller crew.

"There were a lot of cats around outside," Javier said. He wiped his brow with the back of his hand, his chef knife catching a glint of the overhead lights. "They weren't feral or whatever, they just didn't live inside. Maybe they were feral. That means wild, right?"

"I think so," Penelope said. She wiped down her cutting board and grabbed another fish. "I'm not sure what the difference is."

"One of the old ladies in my building would put food out for them so they hung around. She said cats kept the rats away, you know?"

Penelope thought about the blood on Mirabella's head and shivered inwardly.

"Cats are smart," Javier said. "They remember which person brings the food."

"That's what I've heard," Penelope said. "That they're pretty self-sufficient."

"Feral cats are ones that aren't domesticated, or cared for by people," Trevor said as he stepped out of the rear walk-in refrigerator.

Penelope paused and looked at him. Trevor was rarely the one on the team to offer any wisdom or advice.

"Are you getting a cat, Boss?" Trevor asked. He set a tray of beef fillets on the nearest countertop. His arms were tan and his muscles well defined under his t-shirt. He'd pulled his longish blond hair up into a knot on the top of his head today, which Penelope would've thought looked feminine on most men but somehow Trevor pulled it off.

"Well, not really," Penelope said. "My neighbor..." she trailed off, thinking about the scene the night before and how they were all employees of the man in question at the moment. She backtracked and continued, "A cat has been hanging around my house lately, and I might be taking care of it for a while. We have a dog back home in New Jersey, but I've never had a cat before."

"You don't have cats," Javier said, plucking another head of lettuce from the bin on his station and chopping it in half with one arcing blow of his knife. "They have you."

Penelope placed another fish from her bin onto her cutting board and thought about Mirabella in a cage at Animal Control.

With Calvin still in the hospital, and no sign of Brogan, she wondered what Mirabella had witnessed the night before.

"Truck's gassed up and stocked," Francis said as he strolled into the kitchen. "Whenever we're ready."

Penelope glanced at the clock over the door. "Thank you for taking care of it."

"No problem. It will be nice to get back to the beach, right?" Francis said, rubbing his hands together and glancing at the call sheet Bernice had delivered to the kitchen that morning. "Not many mouths to feed today either."

Penelope sliced into the last fish belly, feeling the flesh give way beneath her knife. A cold feeling settled in her stomach as she imagined running the knife over her own wrists like Calvin had apparently done.

She didn't think she'd be able to do it, under any circumstances, even if the world as she knew it seemed like it was coming to an end.

CHAPTER 21

Penelope and her crew set up in a parking lot at the edge of Salacia Beach. It was going to be a short day, according to Chad, and they only had to feed roughly fifty people. Production had a small section of the beach cordoned off for the day's shoot, and the city had given them a three-hour permit. Chad and his crew were motivated to get everything done quickly, but knowing how long he liked to work, Penelope wondered if it would all come together in that amount of time.

Sebastian's stand-in looked every bit the leading man in his shiny suit with an open collared shirt underneath. He was handsome and tan and looked right at home on the beach. Some fans lined the edges of the roped off area, trying to catch a glimpse of filming. "Sebastian" had gone over to talk to a few bikini-clad women when they had first arrived, taking selfies with the group.

A sedan pulled into the parking area and Scarlett emerged, looking out of place in her usual wardrobe of a dark pant suit. She walked toward the lot, a hand shielding her eyes from the sun, her high heels clipping along the asphalt.

"Scarlett," Penelope called to her. She wiped her hands on her apron and walked over to meet her.

Scarlett paused, her eyes hidden behind large round sunglasses. "Penelope. I forgot you were on this set today."

"You're surprised to see me? I've been on this shoot the whole time," Penelope said.

Scarlett grimaced. "I know. Stupid of me. With everything going on, my brain isn't working like it should. I'm picking up a lot of Calvin's projects too and dealing with all of that. He doesn't tell me everything, I've discovered."

"How is your dad?" Penelope asked.

"He's...he'll be okay," Scarlett said. "They're releasing him tomorrow."

"That's good to hear," Penelope said. "Is there anything I can help with?"

"I'm...I'll have to let you know," Scarlett said. "That's nice of you to offer."

"Did he talk to you about what happened?" Penelope asked.

"A little," Scarlett said. A muscle in her jaw twitched and she cleared her throat. "He says it was all a misunderstanding, that he fell and hurt himself after having too much wine."

"What about Brogan?" Penelope asked.

"Calvin is saying all of this happened after Brogan left," Scarlett said with a harsh laugh. "She wasn't even there. They had a fight, she takes off, like she always does...and he made a giant mess of things at the house."

"Oh wow," Penelope said, thinking about the blood and shattered wine glass. She figured it could have happened the way Scarlett had described, especially if Calvin was that overly intoxicated. "Have you spoken to Brogan?"

Scarlett sniffed. "No. But the police have and they're satisfied. There won't be any charges brought against anyone. Which is a relief."

"Well...that is good," Penelope said. "Where is Brogan then?"

"Um, the place she always goes when things get...when they

get..." Scarlett seemed unable to finish her thought, and Penelope realized she was fighting back tears.

"Never mind, I'm asking too many questions," Penelope said. "Come over to the truck and I'll get you a coffee."

Scarlett hesitated at first, then relented. "That sounds great. Iced, if you don't mind." She took a seat under the tent, and Penelope poured her an iced coffee.

"I'm sorry I was asking so much about everything," Penelope said after a few minutes.

"It's fine," Scarlett said with a sigh. She'd already gulped down half of the coffee and was back to her well-composed self. "Brogan has gone off before, after a fight with Calvin. She always comes back. I suppose you probably know by now, they have a pretty boisterous relationship. Lots of yelling."

"I may have heard some of that," Penelope said carefully.

"And for some reason, he insists she's the love of his life," Scarlett said flatly. "I can't see it, he's always been one to spread his love around, but there's no arguing with a fool. And like they say, there's no fool like an old fool."

Penelope reserved comment and gave Scarlett's shoulder a brief squeeze.

"Brogan was the last in a long line of too young, inappropriate girlfriends," Scarlett said, sounding like she had rehearsed the words many times before. "And then he married her. I'm assuming so he'd have someone to take care of him in his old age, or his options had begun to dwindle over the years. I'll give her credit though, she does seem to love him. She signed the prenup without protest, but in return she made sure she was added to his will," Scarlett said, almost like she admired Brogan. "You know she's a year younger than I am, don't you?"

"I wasn't sure," Penelope said. "I knew she was younger than him, of course."

A bubble of laughter erupted from Scarlett, a foreign sound from the usually serious woman Penelope had gotten to know. "Thirty-five years younger than him."

A few of the cast members entered the tent and headed for the coffee station. They'd been talking with each other as they approached but fell silent when they saw Scarlett slouched in the chair, sipping on her iced coffee. Penelope watched them fill their cups and hurry out before she said anything else.

"Where is your mother?" Penelope asked when they were alone again. "Maybe she can help you through this hard time."

"She's gone," Scarlett said, standing up. She set her empty cup down and brushed the lapels of her jacket. "She hasn't been around to help me for a long time."

"I'm sorry," Penelope said.

"Don't be," Scarlett said quickly. The familiar edge had crept back into her voice. "You didn't know. And anyway, I can help Calvin through all of it, and keep things running at the studio until he's better."

"Okay," Penelope said.

"I better check in with Chad, and then I have to head to the next location. Thanks for the coffee." She headed toward Chad, who was talking with some of the crew at the edge of the sand. When he noticed Scarlett approaching, his gestures waved them away and turned toward her with a smile.

"Scarlett?" Penelope called, after she was a few feet away. Scarlett paused and turned back to her. "I was thinking I could take care of Mirabella until...everyone is back home."

"Who?"

"Their cat."

"Oh, right," Scarlett said. "That's fine. I don't know why you'd want to, but I'm sure they'll appreciate it. I got some kind of email from Animal Control that I sent on to Bernice to take care of. Check with her and I'll give whatever permission you need."

"Okay, great," Penelope said. "And thanks."

"Oh, and don't forget about *Knives Out*. The first meeting of the cast and crew is in a couple of days. I'm looking forward to your input."

"I'll be there," Penelope said. She watched her walk toward Chad, the heels of her sensible pumps sinking into the sand, and wondered how she was going to be able to manage everything that was now on her plate.

That day's action on set involved Sebastian's stand-in running through the sand, chasing the stunt double meant to represent Isaac. The setup didn't take long and within an hour of them arriving at the beach, filming was underway.

"Sebastian" ran along the beach, holding a pistol out in front of him, aiming at the stunt man who sprinted ahead of him.

"Stop!" Sebastian shouted breathlessly. Penelope watched them do a few takes then ducked under the canopy to check that everything was in order for lunch. Javier was bent over one of the bins, plucking out small pieces of lettuce, and Trevor was straightening rows of glasses next to him on the drinks table. They had just finished hauling in big containers of tea and water filled with ice and lemon wedges.

"You finding brown lettuce in there?" Penelope asked.

"Nah," Javier said in his quiet tone. "I just like to get rid of the ones that aren't perfect."

"That's what I like about you, Javier," Penelope said. "I never have to worry about your standards."

Javier smiled, and then his shoulders tensed. Chad was

shouting at the actors on the beach as he waved a gun around. Javier looked back down at the lettuce, and continued sorting through it again.

"It's okay if you want to head back to the studio," Penelope said quietly. "We're all set up and the rest of us can take it from here."

"No thank you," Javier assured her. "I've got this."

"Okay," Penelope said, eyeing the precise movements of his fingers. "There's no judgment if you're not fine, though."

"I appreciate that," he said, not looking up at her.

CHAPTER 22

On her way home, Penelope swung through the drive-thru of the In-N-Out Burger and ordered two Double Doubles. She'd become addicted to the popular chain's hamburgers, and wanted to bring one home for Joey to try.

Penelope limited herself to indulging in them once every two weeks at the most. She could definitely have eaten them more often than that, but wanted to keep her waistline in check. Her best friend back home, Arlena, and her fiancé Sam were getting married relatively soon, and Penelope figured she'd be part of the wedding party somehow, which meant trying on dresses and being in a lot of photos. Penelope would also have to be photographed next to Arlena, who had recently been added to one of those Most Beautiful People lists that got circulated from time to time. Yep, a couple of burgers a month while she was in California would have to do. She and Arlena hadn't talked in over a week. She and Sam were scouting out destination wedding spots together and they hadn't been in the same time zone as Penelope in a while. She asked her phone to set a reminder to check in with Arlena soon.

The In-N-Out was next door to a gas station, and Penelope eased up to one of the pumps after making her way through the drive-through. She propped the nozzle in the tank and headed inside to pick up a cold water and some sunscreen.

A small silver bell tinged against the glass door as she

entered, and an aggressively air-conditioned breeze raised the fine blonde hairs on her bare arms. Rubbing them with her hands, Penelope grabbed a few items and set them on the counter. A young clerk with greasy hair and drawn cheeks languidly tapped on the computer screen in front of him.

Penelope's eyes fell on the thin news rack next to the counter. A dozen or so gossip magazines faced out featuring names of celebrities that Penelope had never heard of. The *LA Examiner* newspaper was face up on the stand. "Hollywood Producer Calvin Pope Hospitalized" read the headline. What looked like a professionally taken headshot of Calvin smiled out in black-and-white next to a picture of Brogan Pope and a woman she didn't recognize. Penelope scanned the article and learned she was Calvin's first wife, Robin Pope.

She read to the bottom then flipped the paper over to continue reading beneath the fold. There was a photo of the Pope's house, the roof of Penelope's bungalow barely visible in the photograph. Scanning the article quickly, she came to a dead stop when she read "Robin Pope was presumed to have drowned and declared dead by authorities weeks after she disappeared from Monastery Beach. Mrs. Pope was walking on the beach, accompanied by her husband and daughter when a wave dragged her out to sea, where she presumably drowned. Experienced divers and the Coast Guard searched the cove for several weeks after the incident, but Mrs. Pope's body was never recovered. Robin Pope is survived by her husband, TV and film producer Calvin Pope, and daughter, Scarlett."

"Are you going to buy that or not?" the clerk said in a bored voice. He leaned against the counter on straight arms, his bony shoulder poking up through his rough looking uniform shirt.

"Yes, sorry," Penelope said. She dug in her wallet and handed him a twenty, then stared back down at the article.

Robin Pope was beautiful. Her hair was long and dark, her features soft, her smile warm and sweet. Scarlett looked like her mother around the eyes although her cheekbones were more angular like Calvin's. Opening up the paper, she saw another photograph, this one of Robin holding a young Scarlett propped on her hip, her other arm looped around Calvin's waist. They were standing outside of the studio, and Calvin was pointing at the sign over the door that read Pope Productions.

The clerk banged his cash drawer shut and handed Penelope her change. She folded the paper and stuck it under her arm and took it from him, then hurried back out to the car.

CHAPTER 23

Joey licked his fingers and took another bite of burger, his elbows on the kitchen island. "Oh wow, this is really good." A tomato tried to slide out from under the bun and he tucked it back in.

"I know, right?" Penelope said after swallowing a big bite of hers. "I can't think of anyplace back home that has burgers like this."

"Maybe you can come up with something," Joey said. "Open a burger joint."

"Yeah, I'm not sure about that," Penelope said. "I'm happy with my mobile fine dining job."

"Do you think you'll get more projects out here?" Joey asked, keeping his eyes on his burger.

"I'm not sure," Penelope said. "Maybe. How would you feel about it?"

Joey shrugged half-heartedly. "I'd prefer you to be closer to home, but I wouldn't hold you back from anything you want to achieve."

Penelope set her half-eaten burger down on its wrapper and wiped her mouth with a napkin. "I want to be home with you too."

Joey smiled and met her eyes. "Good." He wadded up his wrapper and tossed it in the bin, then pulled two beers from the fridge behind him and twisted them open. "Tell me about this beach again," he said as he set one down in front of Penelope.

"It's so sad," she said. "Scarlett's mother drowned there apparently." She took a long sip from the bottle then tapped the screen of her iPad that was sitting on the counter. "It's called Monastery Beach, but the locals call it Mortuary Beach because of all of the drowning deaths that happen there."

"Where is it?" Joey asked. He dunked a fry into the tub of ketchup on the counter.

"It's close by," Penelope said. "About a half hour drive down the coast."

"Why would people go swimming in a place called Mortuary Beach?" Joey asked.

"I think it's more for scuba divers, although it's dangerous for them too. A lot of people have been swept off the sand and drowned, not even been in the water," Penelope said. "It sounds like that's what happened to Scarlett's mother. She got hit by a rogue wave while walking on the sand and got pulled under the water."

"Wow," Joey said. He had pulled out his phone and was searching articles about the treacherous spot. "Says here there's an old monastery nearby, which is how the beach got its name."

"Can you imagine watching your mother drown? Scarlett was just a girl."

"No, I can't imagine that," Joey said. "It must have been awful for her and for Calvin to witness. I wonder why they still allow people to swim there."

"I don't know," Penelope said. "Thinking about all of the drownings, and the monastery...it all sounds so eerie."

"Maybe that's what Brogan was talking about when they were arguing the other day when she said she wasn't going to take a swim," Joey said.

"Yikes," Penelope said. "That's a bit of a low blow, isn't it?"

"Pretty low," Joey agreed. "Even though it happened almost twenty years ago, I can't imagine he'd ever get over losing his wife like that."

"Scarlett would've been about ten years old," Penelope mumbled.

"And Brogan not much older than that," Joey said. He swiped a few crumbs into his hand and brushed them into the sink.

"Actually Brogan is a year younger," Penelope said.

"Wow, okay," Joey said with a grimace. "So, what do you want to do now?"

"Go spring Mirabella from cat jail," Penelope said with a sigh.

"Sounds good," Joey agreed. "But later I'd like to take you out to dinner, see more of this Salacia Beach place that stole my love away for the past few months."

CHAPTER 24

Penelope pulled her SUV into the parking lot of the tall glass building that housed the Crime Scene Unit lab and Animal Control.

"I'm going to check in with Clarissa at work," Joey said, holding up his phone. "She was working on something when I left and I want to see how it's going. You okay to go in and get Mirabella on your own?"

"Of course," Penelope said. "I'll be right out, hopefully with a cat."

The reception area of the building was an open space with a prim looking older woman manning a desk that looked as if it had been built with someone much larger in mind. Her gray hair was pinned severely into place and her purple blouse had freshly ironed seams on the sleeves. Her dark-rimmed glasses fit her face perfectly and her lipstick looked professionally applied, a shade darker than Penelope would've chosen, but that somehow looked perfect on the small woman in front of her.

"Can I help you?" the receptionist asked right as Penelope entered, before she'd made it all the way to her desk.

"I'm here to pick up my neighbor's cat," Penelope said.

"Ah, okay, a cat," the woman said, typing something on her keyboard. "There are quite a few of them back there today."

"I was given permission by a member of the family to pick this one up. I've got the release email," Penelope said. She'd stopped into the office on her way out the day before and retrieved it from Bernice.

"It's so good of you, Penelope, really," Bernice had said as they listened to the printer spit out the email. "Scarlett isn't home enough to take care of a cat, and well, you know how Mr. Pope is."

Penelope looked at her curiously. "How he is...what?" she'd asked.

"Oh," Bernice said, waving a hand like she was drying the paint on her nails. "You know, men in general aren't great at taking care of things." When Penelope didn't respond she quickly added, "Of course, maybe he's great with animals. I just got the feeling it was the stepmom's cat and he was just allowing them both to live there with him."

Penelope thanked her for the email and left the office, looking back through the glass door at Bernice one last time as she sat back down and started up her staccato typing on the laptop on her desk. Penelope thought Calvin really liked the cat, but maybe she'd just assumed as much.

"Let's get your paperwork started then," the Animal Control receptionist said. She picked up her phone and punched a few buttons, then handed Penelope a clipboard with a form attached to it.

"Brice?" she said sweetly into the phone. "We have someone out here looking to pick up one of the cats. She was sent by the family." She began to nod then said, "Okay, so send her back then? Great, thank you." She hung up the phone and said to Penelope, "You can go on back and retrieve the cat. Through those doors and then Brice, the tech on duty, will meet you in reception in the third room on the left. Just down that hall."

Penelope handed her the completed form and the woman

buzzed her through the door. She followed her directions and stepped into the designated room off of the hallway. A woman sat behind a glassed-in partition, ignoring Penelope and watching a game show on the television suspended from the ceiling in the waiting area. The door to the right of her opened and a man leaned out, holding on to the door frame as he balanced on one foot. His hair was dyed bright yellow, and his lab coat was stained in a variety of colors, none of which were appealing. He was the opposite in appearance from the primly put together receptionist out front, just as much messy as she was neat.

"Come on back," he said, waving Penelope through the door. She hurried past his bulky frame, being careful not to brush up against his soiled jacket.

"You're here for the long-haired black cat," he said over his shoulder, in more of a statement than a question. "Picked up on Chardonnay Court in Salacia, right?"

"That's correct," Penelope said. She followed him down a corridor, his shoulders wide enough they almost brushed both walls as he passed. They turned into the last room on the right that had a metal exam table in the center and animal cages lining the back wall. They were stacked in three rows, largest on the bottom to the top row of small cages where several cats peeked out through the bars.

"Oh wow," Penelope said. "I wish I could take all of them home."

"We get that a lot," Brice said, running a hand through his spiky, unnaturally-colored hair. Penelope was fascinated by the hue, and wondered where he'd gone to get it done. "Most of the time they are claimed, just here temporarily. But you know...things happen."

Penelope spotted a gerbil on the top row and a snowy white

rabbit in the cage next to it. A dog on the bottom row barked at her a few times while a few others whined that heartbreaking noise that only dogs can make.

"Okay," Brice said, blowing out a loud sigh. "She's going to be on the top row, number...six."

An orange tabby meowed at Brice as he passed by its cage.

"Where did they all come from?" Penelope asked, looking at the rabbit's ruby red eyes.

"From all over," Brice said. "These guys are from the last couple of days. That one's owner," he pointed at the tabby, "died in his sleep, suspected opioid overdose. These dogs on the bottom were left behind by the owners after getting arrested in a drug bust. They were running a distribution ring, so I'm not sure when they'll get home again, if at all."

"What about this guy?" Penelope asked, taking a step closer to the rabbit. His nose twitched, causing his whiskers to quiver.

"He was recovered from the back seat of a drunk driving arrest last night. We have a bunch of birds from that case too in the next room."

"Who takes their rabbit and birds out for drinks?" Penelope asked, her mouth falling open.

"Ha, well, the guy is a magician."

"Oh, that makes more sense," Penelope said.

"Yeah. A magician who had a few too many cocktails after a show down at the Wharf Casino in Salacia."

"That's so...I'm not sure what to say."

"We get all kinds in here," Brice said. "I've heard so many stories you wouldn't even believe."

"I never even thought about what happens to animals after..."

"The unexpected happens," Brice finished her thought. "You know how it is. A lot of people have pets. Even criminals have pets. When stuff goes down, these guys are impacted too. Kids and animals, they suffer the most, if you ask me."

"Where do these animals go after here if the owners are deceased or go to jail?" Penelope asked.

"Either someone like you picks them up," Brice said. "Or," he lowered his voice to a whisper, like he didn't want the animals to her, "Marymount, the no kill shelter near Monterey."

"Well at least they might have a chance there," Penelope said hopefully.

Brice gave her a look like they both knew it was unlikely all of the displaced pets would find a home. But he kindly said, "Sure. There's a chance they'll be adopted." He pulled his phone from the pocket of his lab coat and showed her a photograph. "I've got three dogs of my own, two of them are from here. Lost cause cases where no one was coming to get them." Three large lab-like dogs panted smiles at the screen. In the center of them was a baby snoozing in an infant seat on the floor. The dogs looked like they were standing guard over the baby.

"Aw, so cute," Penelope said.

Brice rubbed his eye with a fist and pocketed his phone. "Thanks. She's eight months old now. We don't' get a lot of sleep. But the dogs, they're great."

Penelope recognized Mirabella's tail sticking through the bars on the top row. "There's Mirabella."

Brice nodded as he checked the number of the cage with the number on his sheet of paper. "Yep, she's the right one." He opened the door of the cage and reached. Mirabella leapt into his arms, not waiting for him to pull her out. "Ha, she's confident."

Brice set a cardboard carrier on the exam table and handed Mirabella to Penelope. The little cat snuggled against Penelope's neck and purred loudly.

"She likes you," he said.

"We've been hanging out some," Penelope said. "She likes to sneak into my house at night."

"Cats are like that," Brice said. "They claim people as their own."

Penelope eased Mirabella into the portable crate and closed the door with Brice's help. Without protest Mirabella curled into the far corner and began licking her paw, waiting to be escorted back home.

"She got some hair on you," Brice said, waving a finger at Penelope's t-shirt.

"I guess I'll have to get one of those lint roller things," Penelope sighed.

"All right then, I just need you to sign here," he said, handing her the clipboard.

"Thanks," Penelope said as she scribbled her name on the sheet. "Did they find anything useful during her examination?"

"I sent in the report yesterday," he said. "Blood, one donor. No trauma to the cat itself. She's good to go."

"Well that's good," Penelope said.

"You'll have to keep her on the Baytril until the prescription runs out," he said, reading from his paperwork. "Her UTI is almost gone, but she shouldn't stop taking it before it's done." She noticed his thumbnail was wrapped with a Band-Aid.

"What happened?" Penelope asked.

"Just a bite," Brice said. "Part of the job here." He peeled it back to show her. His thumbnail was blackened and a small puncture wound pierced the center of his nail.

"Ouch. It wasn't Mirabella who bit you, was it?"

"No, it was a dog last week," Brice said, "It's still healing. I have to give them injections, poke and prod my patients. It happens. Anyway, I sent a copy of the report to the cops, and the veterinary practice in Salacia Beach in case you need to follow up with anything. We always send reports to the vet closest to the owner's address."

"Thanks for everything," Penelope said as she left, the cat carrier securely under her arm. She waved goodbye to the receptionist on the way out and headed for Joey, who was standing outside of the car, finishing up a phone call. She yanked open the door set the carrier on the rear seat of the SUV.

"Everything go okay?" Joey asked.

"Fine," Penelope said as they got back in the car. "Everything good back home?"

"Great," Joey asked. "And while I was at it, I dug up a little more information on the late Mrs. Pope."

"Really?" Penelope asked as she started the car.

"Really," Joey said. "Unfortunately, there's a history of domestic complaints between Calvin and Robin Pope. The cops were called out more than once to break it up. No one was ever charged, but the chief back then called Calvin in, told him he needed to cool off."

"Wow," Penelope said. "I had no idea Calvin could be like that. He's so..."

"Friendly, I know," Joey said. "It's hard to tell what's going on behind closed doors."

"Scarlett had to grow up with that," Penelope said, starting the engine. "It had to have affected her."

"Well, it looks like she and Calvin are close now," Joey said. "Working together, even. They must have worked everything out between them."

Penelope pulled out of the parking lot, checking the rearview mirror to be sure Mirabella's crate hadn't shifted on the seat. The cat's green eyes stared back at hers in the mirror. "I guess they have," Penelope said. "It must have taken a lot for them to come together after all of that, on top of the death of Scarlett's mother."

"Forgiveness is its own reward," Joey said. "It's easier and healthier to forgive than it is to carry around a grudge forever."

"You're right," Penelope said. "Scarlett is a lot stronger than she looks, I guess."

CHAPTER 25

"Jacque is here," Penelope said as they pulled into the driveway back home.

"Jacque?"

"Calvin and Brogan's chef. That's his car." Jacque was in the driveway, retrieving a couple of canvas grocery bags from the rear of his Lexus.

"Well, if the chef is here, the Popes must be coming home," Joey said.

A feeling of dread came over Penelope. She knew she would have to see Calvin and Brogan again, living so close to them and working where she did, but she guessed she wasn't ready to just yet. She was feeling protective of Mirabella, and hoped they'd let her stay with Penelope for a little while at least. "I guess they must be."

Jacque climbed the front porch steps and used a key from his jacket pocket to open the front door.

"I'm going to go say hi," Penelope said.

Joey sighed. "You sure? Don't you want to get her inside and settled?"

"I'll just be a minute," Penelope said, a little defensively.

"No you won't," Joey said. "You're snooping."

"I am not," Penelope said, failing to hide a smile. "I want to see if they have any cat food I can have. I don't know what brand she likes."

"Very nice save," Joey said. "That sounds like a real reason. Although I know you're going to also try and find out what you can about Calvin and Brogan."

"Okay," Penelope said. "You're right. I'm curious. But I think as a caregiver to their pet, I have a right to know when they'll be back."

"Go," Joey said. "I'll get Mirabella settled. Just don't overstay your welcome."

"When do I ever do that?"

Joey laughed under his breath and shook his head as she stepped quickly toward the neighboring house.

"Hi, Jacque," Penelope called from the front foyer. She'd let herself in the front door he'd left open. "It's Penelope from next door."

"Ah, yes, the movie chef," Jacque called down the hall from the kitchen. "Please, come in."

"Thanks," Penelope said, making her way down the hall. Brogan's things were still strewn across the floor and the odor of old wine floated sourly on the air. "I was hoping I could grab a few of Mirabella's things. I'm watching her until—"

"*Oui, oui*, until…I know until what," Jacque said grimly. "The woman from the office sent me here to clean out everything that has spoiled the last few days, and to prepare something fresh for Mr. Pope to eat when he gets home."

"So he'll be here soon, then," Penelope said.

"From what she said, yes," Jacque said.

"You mean Scarlett?"

"No, the woman with the strange name at his office," Jacque said.

"Bernice?"

"*Oui*, that is the one."

Penelope didn't think Bernice was a particularly funny name, but maybe it was in France where Jacque was from.

"He will be released in the morning, and then...he'll be here, I guess. The...what do you call it...mandatory observation period is done."

"That's good news for Calvin," Penelope said. "I'm sure he's anxious to get out of the hospital."

"Yes, well none of us like to be there," Jacque said, looking around the kitchen. "Look at the mess they have made. The house cleaners are on their way too. Although I told Bernice—" he pronounced her name so the last part sounded like "ice," "—I am not supervising any kind of maid service. I'm a chef, only here to cook for my clients. I am not house manager."

"Of course," Penelope said. "I'm sure she understands."

"You think so? I don't know. Anyway, the cleaners, they are earning their money this week for sure. Look at this mess." He waved a disgusted hand in the air.

Penelope saw that the wine spill and shattered glass were still on the floor next to the dining room, and the plates had been left on the table, the food rotting.

"It's pretty bad," Penelope said. "Maybe I should open the doors, air the place out?"

"Good idea," Jacque said. "The smell in here is terrible. I'm sure the refrigerator isn't much better." He cursed under his breath in French as Penelope went to the doors and opened them. The ocean air was an immediate relief, diffusing the rotten smells from inside the house.

Even though Penelope had been in the house many times, she began to see things around her she hadn't noticed before. There was a framed painting on the wall, which looked to Penelope like an original Georgia O'Keefe print of one of her famous flowers. A vase with a wilted bouquet drooped in the center of the foyer table, the flowers giving off the thick odor of decay.

"I think there's some cat food in the pantry," Jacque said, interrupting her thoughts. "Go ahead and check."

"Okay," Penelope said. She went to the pantry and opened the door. After hunting for a few seconds, she found a stack of cat food cans on the top shelf. Penelope set them on the counter then continued looking for more, or a container of dry food. She had no idea when Mirabella usually ate, or what she liked. She found a small plastic container of dry cat food and set it next to the stack of cans.

"Do you know if Brogan will be home too?" Penelope asked, as casually as possible.

Jacque shook his head. "No, but she usually returns after a week's time, you know, after one of their...episodes. It's how you say...*leur chemin?*"

"I'm sorry I don't know that phrase," Penelope said.

"Ah, it's 'their way,' I guess is how you'd say it in English."

"This is the first incident I've been aware of. I didn't realize it was a regular occurrence with them," Penelope said.

"*Oui*, yes," Jacque said. "*Ordinaire.*"

"Where does she go usually?"

"Mrs. Pope owns a flat," Jacque said with a disinterested shrug. "It was her residence before the two of them were married. She held onto it, she said once, to have a place for friends to stay or to rent it on one of those websites." He shivered slightly at the thought.

"Like FlatShare.com?"

"I'm sure I wouldn't know," Jacque said. "Anyway, she goes there. I brought her some meals one time. I charged three times the rate to go out of my way. I have other clients, I told her, and my schedule is not a free for all."

"Is it close by?" Penelope asked.

"On the north end of the beach, in the Maison. It's an old mansion divided up into a few units. It's a nice place," Jacque said. "I can see why she wants to hang onto it. The way the shoreline curves in like a 'C,' you can almost see us here from there, if you have a telescope."

"I suppose it's good for her to have a place to go when things get..."

"The way they get," Jacque said with a nod.

"I did pick up on some tension between them from time to time when I was visiting. And I overheard an argument the other morning."

"Some people prefer to live their lives at the edge of a fire," Jacque said. He began removing items from the canvas grocery bags he'd set on the counter. "I prefer my home on the chilly side. I'd rather my husband bore me to death than live with explosions all of the time."

"I know what you mean," Penelope said.

"Don't get me wrong, we are not a boring pair, he is exciting in his own way. But this—" he waved a box of organic spaghetti at the mess on the floor, "—this is not what you want for a marriage."

"I agree."

"Are you married?" Jacque said, eyeing her naked ring finger.

"No," Penelope said. "Not yet."

Jacque gave her a smile. "Trust me, find someone who is steady, and has control of their passions. Even if you are bored sometimes. That's the key to a long-term union. Don't tell the Popes I said any of this, of course. To each their own as they say."

"I won't say anything," Penelope said. "Chef's honor."

Jacque hummed an unfamiliar song as he finished unpacking the grocery bags. "It's amazing what couples will talk about, and fight about, right in front of the people who work for them. It's almost like they think we don't have ears at all."

"It happens to all of us," Penelope said, picking up one of the tins with a furry white cat with green eyes on the label. "You become invisible to your employers after a while." The wine stain had seeped between the wooden slats on the floor. Penelope wondered if they'd have to buff it out and refinish the floor.

"But we do hear them, yes?" Jacque said. "And as you probably know, if you want to work in anyone else's kitchen again, you keep yourself to yourself and stay quiet. You become known as a staff member who gossips, you'll never work in a home again."

"There's nothing saying we can't listen, though," Penelope said. "Sometimes it can be very revealing, to be a fly on the wall."

"Correct," Jacque said. "As long as you don't get swatted."

Penelope smiled at him.

"That's all they have for cat food, I think." Jacque pulled his phone from his back pocket and opened up a grocery ordering app. "I'll add more to the list for next week. And I have to remember to take these other things off."

"What other things?" Penelope asked, glancing at the list of items on his screen.

"You know how clients get sometimes," Jacque says. "Especially out here in health-conscious California, with all the crazy diets. First Mrs. Pope quit drinking. Okay, fine, that's healthy. Now she's banning me from buying coffee, lunchmeat, tuna, mackerel, grassy sprouts, and soft cheeses. I've seen the woman eat an entire wheel of brie by herself. And now I have to soak all the produce with this organic solution she created for me. I mean, what kind of crazy diet is this?"

As Penelope watched him delete the items he mentioned from the list, something dawned on her. "Thanks for the food, and the conversation," Penelope said. "I better get home. Mirabella is probably starving."

"Okay," Jacque said. "Thanks for taking care of her. They ask me to feed her sometimes if they're gone overnight...I certainly didn't spend all that money at culinary school to make a cat's dinner. Not that she isn't cute, but you know what I mean. It's a bit beneath my skill set."

"I hear you." Penelope said goodbye to Jacque and headed out the front door. She paused on the front porch and wondered how far along Brogan Pope was in her pregnancy.

CHAPTER 26

"What do you mean, pregnant?" Joey asked. "How do you figure? She certainly isn't showing yet."

"I can tell from the food," Penelope said. "She gave Jacque a list of things not to bring into the house, and they are all the ones they you to avoid in the early months of pregnancy."

"How are you so sure about that?" Joey asked.

"Remember the movie I was working on when we first met, back in New Jersey?"

"How could I forget," Joey said with a smile.

"The cinematographer was pregnant. In her first trimester. She gave me a list of foods she was told to avoid by her doctor. I looked it up back then to see why they were excluded. You wouldn't think of all of them, so I was curious."

"Interesting," Joey said.

Joey opened a can of Mirabella's food and spooned some onto a saucer, then set it on the floor. "Well, congratulations to them, I guess," he said sarcastically.

"Maybe that's what they were fighting about. Maybe she's having second thoughts about everything," Penelope said. "Their marriage seems far from stable."

"We don't know for sure she's pregnant," Joey said.

"But..."

"But you're probably right, and she is," Joey agreed. "And

from what this Jacque says they fight a lot. But they are happy most of the time, right?"

"Calvin is in the hospital on a psych hold after hurting himself, and Brogan has run off, not for the first time, after they trashed their house."

"Okay," Joey said with a sigh. "I guess I was trying to be optimistic. I don't want to think about a kid being born into the middle of that either."

"Not to mention Brogan hasn't checked in with anyone," Penelope said, watching Mirabella daintily tuck into her food. "Wouldn't she be worried about Calvin, and Mirabella?" Penelope asked. "If you were in the hospital, I'd be beside myself, especially if I was pregnant with your child."

"If she's thinking of leaving, she might not. Or had something to do with him ending up there. Maybe she's beyond caring," Joey said. "Maybe she wants a new life with just herself and the baby."

"Joey, we're not going to end up hating each other, are we?" Penelope asked quietly. "We're not going to just quit caring about each other, right?"

"Are you kidding me?" Joey asked. He pulled her to him and hugged her roughly. "We're nothing like them, Penny. I'm going to spend my life taking care of you and caring about you every day. I'd give my life for yours, you know that."

Penelope felt a wave of emotion and hugged him back even harder.

"Hey," Joey said. "Let's get out of here. I found the perfect place on the boardwalk for us to have dinner. We need a break from all things Pope, don't you think?"

"Yes," Penelope said. "That's a great idea."

CHAPTER 27

Penelope and Joey held hands as they strolled down the boardwalk at Salacia Beach Wharf, live music drifting on the air from one of the cafes as they passed by. The tang of fried seafood mixed with the salty night air made Penelope's mouth water as they made their way to the restaurant Joey had chosen in the center of the row. She had changed into a pale pink sundress and a jean jacket. The heat of the day had slipped away and the air felt cool against her skin.

Joey squeezed her hand. "You look beautiful."

"Thank you," Penelope said. "You clean up well too."

"Here's the place. Beachside Café," Joey said, leading her to an open-air restaurant with a line of tables outside on the boardwalk.

"This looks perfect," Penelope said. Beachside Café was lined with dark wood and decorated to look like the interior of a vintage ship.

The hostess led them to a table outside with a view of the boardwalk and the ocean beyond. When the waitress arrived, Joey ordered a bottle of white wine, which they sipped as they scanned through the menus.

"Everything sounds delicious," Penelope said, setting her menu down on the table.

"What are you going to order?" Joey said.

"A lot more evenings like this one," Penelope said.

"I think we can arrange that," Joey said.

"And the swordfish," Penelope teased.

"Penny, I wanted to—"

A piece of silverware clattered to the floor inside and Penelope looked inside. "Hey," Penelope said. "I know her."

"Who?" Joey asked, swiveling around to look. A woman was sitting at a table for two next to the bar, drinking a martini, her back to them.

"I'm almost positive that's Bernice from work. The administrator in the office," Penelope said. "It's dark but it could be her."

Joey sighed. "And here I was hoping I'd get you away from work for a while."

Penelope brought her attention back to Joey. "I'm sorry. You're right. What were you saying?"

"Nothing," Joey said.

"You were saying something," Penelope said. "Please tell me."

"Okay," Joey said after a pause. "Penny, I want to ask you something very important."

"Have you decided on your appetizers?" An overly enthusiastic waitress had appeared out of nowhere next to their table. Joey closed his eyes for a beat then smiled at her.

"I'll have the seared Ahi tuna, please," he said.

"Are you okay with the spicy sauce with that?" she asked perkily. "It's pretty spicy so I always ask everyone, are you okay with it being really spicy, because I don't want you to be disappointed."

"Spicy is good," Joey said, not unkindly. "However it comes is fine with us."

"And I'll have the calamari," Penelope said. "Any heat of the sauce is fine."

"Awesome," the waitress said, then bopped away.

"You were saying..." Penelope said, taking a sip of her wine. Joey had chosen a crisp Sauvignon Blanc that paired well with the cool salty breeze and their choice of appetizers.

"Yes," Joey said. The tension had gone out of his face and he smiled, helping her to relax too. "You know how I feel about you, Penny. About us. And I want to know—"

"Penelope?" Scarlett approached their table from the boardwalk. It was the first time Penelope had seen her in a dress, and not in one of her signature pant suits.

"Scarlett, hi," Penelope said. "Joey, I don't think you've met Scarlett Pope."

Joey stood up from his seat and shook her hand. "It's nice to meet you. I'm sorry about what happened to your father."

"Thanks. It's nice to meet you too," Scarlett said. Her eyes past their table toward the bar.

"Are you here to meet Bernice?" Penelope asked, following her gaze. "I think that's her at that table over there."

"What? No," Scarlett said. "Bernice is here?"

Penelope pointed at the table. The small woman with the short black hair was engrossed with something on her phone, her martini glass half empty, her back to them.

"I'm not sure that's her. Besides, I get enough of Bernice at the office," Scarlett said with an uncharacteristic laugh. "Just kidding, that sounds mean. Bernice is wonderful. I just meant, who wants their boss hanging around on their night off, am I right? You're probably thinking the same thing."

Penelope kept quiet, unused to seeing Scarlett outside of work and so talkative.

"I can't join you anyway, I'm heading to a show." Scarlett waved vaguely down the boardwalk. No one had asked her to join, but it was good to know she wasn't expecting an invitation.

Joey sat back down and took a sip of his wine.

"How's your father doing?" Penelope asked.

Scarlett nodded. "Just fine. He's a tough old guy. I will have to talk to him about cutting back on his drinking from now on. But let's keep that between us. I'm only saying that because you saw how things...can get."

"I'm sure he appreciates your support, Scarlett," Penelope said encouragingly.

"Sure," she said, then pulled her phone from her purse and glanced at the screen. "I have to run, don't want to be late."

"See you tomorrow then?" Penelope said.

Scarlett tapped on her phone and stuck it back in her bag. "Yes," Scarlett said. "See you then. Must run now." She pulled her shawl tighter around her shoulders and continued on down the boardwalk.

"Okay," Penelope said, turning back to Joey. "Where were we?"

"I've got your appetizer," the waitress said, with more enthusiasm than was necessary. "It's spicy, remember. Are you all set to order dinner now?"

Penelope and Joey made their dinner selections, each heartily approved of by their waitress. After she'd gone again, Joey picked up his fork and dug into the seared tuna.

"I think we might finally have a quiet minute," Penelope said.

Joey laughed and gave her a smile. "You know what? Let's talk about it when we get home."

"Are you sure?" Penelope asked.

"Very sure," Joey said. "In the meantime, a toast to you, the most interesting, ambitious, and beautiful woman I've ever met."

Penelope blushed and clinked glasses with him.

* * *

Penelope scraped the bottom of the dish with her spoon, scooping up the last of the mango sorbet. Their waitress had assured them that Beachside Café was famous for their fresh fruit sorbet, which was made in house to order.

"Give her a big tip," Penelope said after she'd placed the check discreetly on the corner of the table.

Penelope had gotten up to use the ladies' room in between their main course and dessert, and noticed that the table where the woman she thought was Bernice had been sitting was empty. Penelope hadn't seen her leave, but assumed she must have slipped out unnoticed by her in one of the many waves of arriving and departing guests. Beachside Café had gotten much busier just in the time that they'd been there. A band was setting up in the back of the bar, bringing in dozens more patrons.

When they got back to the beach house Penelope and Joey were so exhausted from their wonderful meal and long walk on the beach afterwards, that they fell into bed and were fast asleep within minutes. Mirabella curled up on the bedspread between them, snuggling against their legs.

CHAPTER 28

Penelope got to the studio early the next morning and headed to the office to check in with Bernice. She wasn't sure where she was supposed to report for the first day of the *Knives Out* production, but figured it would be in one of the conference rooms.

Bernice wasn't at her desk, which was unusual. Normally she was the first one in and was on her second cup of coffee before anyone else arrived at the studio. The hallway outside her office was quiet too and for a minute Penelope wondered if she'd come in on the wrong day. Then she remembered running into Scarlett the night before, and her saying they'd see each other at work the next day, and figured she was just early.

It felt strange leaving for work out of her chef clothes that morning, but she was just going to be sitting in on a day of meetings with no cooking involved. She'd decided on a comfortable pair of dark jeans and silky blouse. Although she looked nice, she felt like she was playing dress up at the office.

Penelope stepped inside the office and noticed the door to Scarlett's suite was ajar.

"Fine. Have it your way. Just get it done," Bernice said as she came through the door and pulled it closed behind her, a little more forcefully than necessary. When she saw Penelope standing in front of her desk, she stopped short and put a hand to her throat. Her ears turned pink under her dark black pixie cut, but she recovered quickly.

"You gave me a start," Bernice said with a laugh. "I didn't think anyone was in yet."

"Sorry. Is Scarlett in her office?"

"No," Bernice said, glancing back at the door. "I was just using the phone in there to call the maintenance crew. One of the sinks in the men's room is broken. No water, so..." She wore a skintight pencil skirt with a sleeveless turtleneck in a deep eggplant color.

"That's a pain," Penelope said, glancing at the phone on Bernice's desk. "I'm sitting in on the *Knives Out* casting meeting today, and at first I thought I got the date wrong—"

"No, it's this morning. We set up the conference room for you all last night. You can wait in there if you like, Scarlett will be in shortly. There's coffee in there, and we'll have breakfast brought in for you all, and lunch when you're ready for it."

"A long day then," Penelope said.

Bernice nodded and stood behind her desk.

"Hey, I think I saw you last night, down on the wharf. At Beachside Café?"

Bernice twisted her lips into a half smile. "I don't think so. I was home in front of the television binging...both *The British Bakeoff* and a pint of ice cream. Don't tell anyone," she added, running her hand down her flat stomach.

"Ha," Penelope said. "Well, I'm glad I didn't wander over and embarrass myself then. There was a woman there who from the back looked just like you."

Bernice shook her head and pulled out her chair. "I don't get out much anymore. Oh, don't forget to log in your hours today. You're getting executive-level pay for this project. You have to enter a different code on the sheet."

"Okay, will do," Penelope said. They heard the door in the

next office open and close and someone moving around on the other side of the wall.

"That'll be Scarlett," Bernice said. "You should probably get to your meeting." Bernice opened her laptop and started typing, her fingers flying rapidly across the keyboard. Penelope saw herself out and headed for the conference room, passing by Scarlett's suite on the way. A briefcase and jacket had been thrown across the visitor's chair and a door in the far corner was open, the edge of the bathroom sink just visible.

Continuing to the end of the hallway, Penelope came to the large conference room and went inside.

"Good morning, Penelope."

Calvin Pope was at the head of the table, his hands folded in front of him, the familiar grin on his face.

CHAPTER 29

"Calvin!" Penelope said. "What are you doing here?"

"My name's on the building," Calvin said. "Where else would I be?" A small square bandage was visible just below his hairline, but his floppy bangs hid it for the most part. He wore a long-sleeved shirt, buttoned at the cuffs, but Penelope couldn't see any thick bandages there either. Calvin looked fine, in stark contrast to the man she'd seen on the stretcher in his house a few nights ago.

"How are you feeling?" Penelope asked. She pulled out a chair close to the door, but he motioned for her to sit next to him.

"I'm doing all right, thanks for asking."

"We were so worried about you," Penelope said.

"I've told Calvin he can't carry on like that anymore," Scarlett said from the doorway. She was back in a suit this morning, a deep dark blue with a low-cut white top underneath.

"You all know I can take care of myself," Calvin said. "But I have promised my daughter I'll pump the breaks on overindulging for the time being."

Scarlett sat at the opposite end of the table and shook her head. "Poor Penelope had to see you in that condition, too. You should thank her for calling the ambulance. Brogan didn't have the decency—"

Calvin held up his hand, cutting her off. "Let's not bring Brogan into this. Penelope, thank you for coming to my rescue. I'm forever in your debt. I am mortified you had to see me like that, but I promise on my honor I will make it up to you."

"It's fine," Penelope said. "I'm just glad you're okay."

"Is this the culinary competition meeting?" A man stuck his head in the doorway and looked around the room.

"Yes, come in."

The room soon filled up with the executive production team for *Knives Out*. Once everyone had gotten settled, poured themselves coffee, and selected breakfast items from the continental spread on the sideboard, Scarlett called the meeting to order.

"Thank you all for being here and for being a part of this new Pope Production venture," she began. "You've each been hand selected by me and my father for the team because we think you each bring a unique perspective, and that together we will build something fun that will catch fire with viewers."

Penelope had to admit she was excited to be involved in the show. Scarlett went around the room and introduced all of the team members, which consisted of a casting agent, a seasoned reality TV director, three scriptwriters, a food stylist, and Penelope, who was introduced as the senior culinary consultant.

Bernice knocked twice and then opened the door. "Everything okay in here?"

"Fine," Scarlett said without looking up. "You can have them clear everything down when we take our break at ten, and refresh the coffee please."

Bernice ducked out and closed the door behind her. She must have known Calvin was coming in that morning. She didn't seem surprised to see him sitting at the table.

"If you'll all open the green folder in front of you," Scarlett said, "we can start making our decisions on contestants."

The next hour was spent on reviewing and discussing the different applicants who were vying for a spot on the show. Penelope was impressed with some of the résumés of the chefs. Several of them had attended top culinary schools, and many had worked at well-regarded restaurants around the country. Flipping over the last page, she laughed out loud in surprise.

"Someone you know?" Scarlett asked, glancing at the headshot they were all holding.

"He's one of my chefs," Penelope said, holding up the entry form. "Trevor Barksdale, we just worked on the *Severed Lies* set together."

"I thought he looked familiar," Scarlett said. "Well, he made the initial cut and was vetted by Trish's team, so he's in the pile."

Trish was the casting agent who had compiled the thirty applicants they were considering. During the introductions she'd told the group over two hundred chefs had applied for a spot on the show and her team had narrowed it down to the choices in front of them.

"And his CV checked out," Trish said. "He actually went to the school he listed, worked where he said he did." She leaned toward Penelope and muttered, "Everyone lies about their experience these days. We double and triple check every reference."

"Good to know," Penelope said.

"Everyone in this stack has viewer appeal and the cooking chops to back them up," Trish said.

"Viewer appeal?" Penelope asked.

"Their appearance will translate well to TV," Trish said. "And they're all physically capable of the exertion they'll be put under per the show concept, cooking for a minimum of ten hours an episode."

"What are your thoughts on Trevor as a cheftestant, Penelope?" Calvin asked.

Penelope glanced at Trevor's headshot. "I don't have anything negative to say about him at all. He's charming, hardworking, knows his food."

"Good," Scarlett said. "He goes in the maybe pile."

"Can we get their faces up on the screen?" Calvin asked, reaching forward to press a button on a large remote on the table. A monitor mounted on the wall behind him came to life and he swung his chair around while the rest of them adjusted their seats to get the best view of the screen.

Calvin pressed buttons on the remote, pausing between each photo of the chefs.

"She's good," Calvin said. "That one goes in the yes pile."

"Based on...?" Scarlett asked, flicking her eyes at the back of her father's head.

"Look at her. I can already see the *Knives Out* logo blazed across the front of her shirt." He kept the image of the attractive young chef, Ella Banks, on the screen. Several members of the team pulled her sheet from the pile and jotted notes. Ella had trained in Paris and had a decent résumé, the one restaurant in San Francisco she'd worked at was part of a larger chain managed by a pair of celebrity chefs. Ella was less experienced and about ten years younger than most of the other candidates, but it seemed she was starting out on a great career path, so Penelope had no issue with Calvin's choice.

Scarlett chewed her bottom lip and turned to the next page in her packet. "I get next pick."

"Fine by me," Calvin said. "I can play fair."

Forty-five minutes later, they'd narrowed the applicants down to a diverse group of twelve contestants, six men and six women.

"Culinarily speaking," Penelope said, "this is a dream team."

"Who should be our villain?" one of the writers asked. The three members of the writing team had offered the least input during the selection process, but now that the team was set, they were busy making notes on the individual entry forms.

"Villain?" Penelope asked.

"Of course," the writer said, giving Penelope a look as if what he'd said should be completely obvious. "You've got your villain, love interest, narrator, mentor...the character roles for the show."

"Viewers respond to characters," his partner said, not unkindly. "If we have a big bunch of boring vanilla people with no conflict or who don't bond with each other, we won't get the ratings."

"Ratings are good!" Calvin said, too loudly.

"Where are the psych evals?" the third writer asked Trish. She pulled a file from her bag and sorted through it, pulling twelve reports from the stack. The writers divided the pile between them and began reading, turning pages rapidly.

"Anything to be concerned about from the background checks?" Scarlett asked.

"Nothing criminal," Trish said. "No drug arrests or violent histories, per Pope Production regulations." Scarlett looked at her father from across the table. "We cut twenty-five applicants the first day after the criminal checks came back. Mostly drug related charges."

"Any minor offenses?" one of the writers asked.

"A few. Nothing that goes against regulations. This one," Trish held up the photo of Ella, the attractive young woman Calvin had chosen first, "had a DUI several years ago, but that falls within the parameters of an acceptable criminal past."

Scarlett rolled her eyes. Calvin looked at the pretty chef's picture again and appeared even more interested in her. "Nothing wrong with enjoying a few drinks once in a while."

"I think we have enough here to get started," the first writer said, pushing his wire-rimmed glasses back onto the bridge of his nose. "We'll start building the basic storylines and have them ready for the first kitchen audition."

"I'm sorry I'm asking so many questions," Penelope began, "but just so I'm on the same page, they're going to audition for a spot in the kitchen?"

"Yes," Scarlett said. "These dozen are our preliminary picks, but we have to see how they play on camera before they're finally chosen. Your input is going to be a part in the choosing of candidates, after you see them in action."

"Okay," Penelope said. "Got it."

"I think that's enough for today," Calvin said. "Give this pile a call back and if any of them aren't available, pull from our B-list choices."

Trevor had made the first cut. Penelope knew he would be excited to get the call back.

"Good meeting, everyone," Scarlett said. "We'll see all of you tomorrow for the screen tests in the kitchen at noon. Trish, can I see you in my office?"

Penelope lingered behind as the room cleared out with Calvin bringing up the rear.

"How are you feeling?" Penelope asked when it was just the two of them left in the room.

"I'm doing well," Calvin said. "It's good to be back at work."

"If I can help you at all, just let me know," Penelope said. "Joey and I are right next door."

"Thanks, that's very nice of you," Calvin said. The healthy color had returned to his face but his smile didn't quite reach his eyes. There was a lingering sadness there just beneath the surface.

"How is Brogan?" Penelope asked.

The sadness hardened, and Penelope saw a brief flash of hatred cross his features before he shook his head and choked out an empty laugh.

"Ah, my lovely wife," Calvin said. "Soon to be ex-wife, I'm afraid."

"Oh," Penelope said. "I'm so sorry." She wasn't completely surprised at the news, thinking about the scene at the Pope's house a few nights before, but it was still a bit of a shock to hear him say it so plainly.

"Turns out I'm terrible at choosing spouses," Calvin said. "It's my fatal flaw."

"Mr. Pope?" Bernice was in the doorway, waving to Calvin. "There's a call for you. I tried to put them off but they're insisting."

"Be right there," he said. He moved past Penelope stiffly, as if sitting in the chair for the morning hadn't agreed with his aging bones. "We'll talk soon," he said to her as he passed.

CHAPTER 30

"They're splitting up," Penelope said. She and Joey were standing face to face in the shallow end of the pool. They'd just finished racing each other through ten laps from end to end, and Penelope was still catching her breath. She'd finished just before Joey, who swore he hadn't let her win. Mirabella had run alongside on the patio, meeting them at the edges when they came up for air.

"Shh," Joey said, tilting his head at the house next door. "The glass walls have ears."

"I'm pretty sure Calvin is still at the studio," Penelope said. "I only saw Jacque's car there when I got home. But you're right about keeping our voices low."

They got out of the pool and toweled off, their bathing suits dripping onto the patio from their chaise lounges. Mirabella perched at the end of Joey's chaise, blinking at him from between his feet.

"She's taken a real liking to you," Penelope said, rubbing her hair with the towel.

"We've been spending a lot of time together," Joey said. "Napping, reading, hanging out by the pool."

"I hope you're not too bored," Penelope said. "I know I've been leaving you home to go to work a lot."

"Are you kidding?" Joey said. "This is my vacation. I'm in full on relaxation mode. Although I kind of want to see you do your judging thing in the kitchen at the studio tomorrow. Would you mind if I came in with you, or would that make you uncomfortable?"

"I'd love for you to be there," Penelope said. "This is a whole new experience for me, so I could use a friend in my corner."

A faint knocking came from inside the house. Mirabella sprang up and trotted to the sliding glass doors.

"It sounds like someone is at the door," Joey said. "I'll get it."

Penelope sat up and watched Joey go inside. A minute later a flustered looking Jacque was outside on the patio.

"...I wouldn't ask except it's an emergency," Jacque was saying to Joey. "The biggest emergency ever!"

"Jacque, what's wrong?" Penelope said, springing up from the lounge chair. "Is Calvin hurt?"

"Oh, he's fine. I think. He's not home," Jacque said. He held his phone up, showing it to Joey. "I have to get to the hospital. It's time."

"Time for what?" Joey asked, trying to read the message on the screen.

"Our baby is coming," Jacque said. "Two weeks early! Our surrogate started having contractions this morning, and when she called, they told her to get to the hospital right away. My son is about to be born!"

"That's amazing!" Penelope said. "Do you need us to give you a ride?" She still wasn't sure why Jacque had stopped over to tell them his news.

Jacque shook his head. "No, but I have a week's worth of Mrs. Pope's food prepared next door. It's all sitting out on the counter. The doctor is saying things are underway...if I don't leave now, I might miss the birth. My husband is texting me every thirty seconds to get there! I don't have time to pack everything and deliver it to Mrs. Pope."

Joey put a hand on Jacque's shoulder. "We'll handle things here. You go and be with your family."

Jacque laughed and his eyes glassed over with tears. "Family. *Ma famille. Je vu remercie*...I can't even...just...thank you."

Jacque handed a set of keys to Joey, explaining the first one was to the house next door and the one with the red mark was to Brogan's condo ten miles away in Salacia Beach's north end.

"You told me about her place already," Penelope said. "We'll take everything to her. We're so happy for you—I hope all goes well!"

CHAPTER 31

Penelope and Joey changed their clothes quickly and went next door, making sure Mirabella had food and water in her dishes and the doors were locked behind them.

A large wooden bowl of mixed greens sat drying on the counter, surrounded by a variety of colorful fruits and vegetables.

"He finished chopping everything, we just have to put it together," Penelope said, eyeing Jacque's knife skills. "Pretty straightforward. Then I'll finish off the salmon from the fridge and we can go."

Joey began assembling the salads in the containers Jacque had left on the edge of the island while Penelope seared off the fish. As he put the lid on the last salad, his phone pinged in his back pocket.

"Huh," Joey said.

"What's up?" Penelope asked. Her back was to him as she removed the final piece of salmon from the griddle and set it on a cutting board next to the stove so it could cool before she packed it up.

"I just got a text from Clarissa," Joey said. Clarissa and Joey's partnership back home in New Jersey had started out on the rocky side, but they soon formed a solid bond. Joey wasn't always effusive with praise, but he'd been very complimentary of

Clarissa over the past year. "She sent me a link." He clicked on it and an article opened on the screen. "The gun used in the Sebastian Beauregard shooting has been traced back to Heston Berkley."

"The actor?" Penelope said, looking over his shoulder.

"Heston Berkley," Joey read out loud, "famous for his many tough guy movie roles as well as his extensive collection of firearms, reported the gun stolen from his Los Angeles home over two years ago. Police were able to recover the serial number from the weapon through scientific means after an attempt to remove the number through filing and application of acid."

"So," Penelope said, "someone stole a gun from Heston Berkley and then used it hundreds of miles away in Salacia Beach to murder Sebastian Beauregard?"

"That's what it looks like," Joey said. "I caught a case last month where the gun had made its way from Chicago. There were two other homicides connected to it, too. There's a network out there, guns are bought and sold illegally, traded for drugs. It's very common." He read the rest of the article, which was a recap of the shooting, and Mr. Berkley's various statements about responsible gun ownership through the years. When he finished reading, he said, "Sebastian's body will be flown back to Australia soon. The family is eager to have him home so they can plan his funeral."

"Family," Penelope said. She thought about what his family must be going through back home. Sebastian had arrived in the U.S. with so much potential and had already come so far in his career, only to be cut down before it really got started.

"Can I see that?" Penelope asked, pausing to look at the screen. There were a few pictures of Sebastian throughout the article, and one of what she assumed were his parents. "Who is that?" she asked. A fine-featured woman with a scarf tied over her hair and sunglasses on was pictured heading into a police station.

"The caption says it's his wife," Joey said. "Did you know Mr. Universe was married?"

"I sure didn't," Penelope said. "He never mentioned it once. In fact, he bragged about his...girlfriends, all of the time."

"What a guy," Joey said, focusing on the food in front of him.

"I feel like I've seen her before," Penelope said, enlarging the picture. "Sara Charles is her name."

"How is that possible?" Joey asked. "She's on the other side of the world."

"Maybe she's behind what happened to Sebastian," Penelope said. "Maybe she couldn't take his cheating."

"Maybe," Joey said. "The spouse is the first suspect."

"I remember reading about Heston's LA mansion in a magazine once," Penelope said, handing him back the phone. "It's enormous. He hosts a huge gala every winter, like a costume ball, to raise money for some gun advocacy groups. The costumes were really elaborate. I wonder what they served for dinner."

"Your mind always goes to food," Joey said.

"I know," Penelope said. "Speaking of, let's get this stuff packed in the cooler and delivered."

CHAPTER 32

Penelope and Joey lugged the large white cooler from the back of her SUV to the front door of the condo.

"I've got the key," Penelope said, after they set it down on the front porch of the Maison. The units had been designed so none of them shared an entrance, so while there were six units in the large structure, it felt more like a private residence.

Joey knocked on the door and they waited for a response. After a minute he knocked again.

"Let's just slip in and get it put away," Penelope said. Using the key to open the door, they stepped inside. A cool ocean breeze swept past them from the back of the house, where a large picture window overlooking the beach was open.

"Nice place," Joey said.

"I can see why she wanted to hold onto it," Penelope said.

"A good decision, it turns out," Joey said.

They passed a hallway on the left which led to a powder room to the right and three doors, which Penelope assumed were the bedrooms.

The kitchen was small but functional, with another large window with a view of the beach below. "You can just see their house," Penelope said, pointing at the glass.

Joey took a quick look then started unloading the cooler he'd set on the floor in front of the refrigerator.

"You might have to revise your pregnancy theory," Joey

said, after having a look inside.

"What do you mean?"

"There's just a six pack of beer in here," Joey said. "Two are missing. And no food."

"That's why we're here," Penelope reminded him. She pulled out a couple of bottles of water to make room on the top shelf. "Let's stack everything neatly for her."

"What the hell are you doing in here?" a man said from behind them.

Penelope jumped, dropping a water bottle on the floor. Joey spun around, reaching for the small of his back where his off-duty weapon would normally be, but he'd left it in the glove compartment before they'd headed inside.

"Isaac?" Penelope said. "What are you doing here?"

"Wait, who are you?" Isaac held one of the beer bottles in his hand, and held the other one palm up in a shrug.

"Penelope from the set," she said. "Catering?"

"Oh," Isaac said, his confused look falling away, then coming back. He sneezed suddenly and violently, then continued. "But...why are you here again?" He had on a loose pair of basketball shorts and no shirt, his bare feet rocking slightly on the carpet.

Joey turned back around and began loading the food containers into the refrigerator.

"Brogan's chef got called to the hospital unexpectedly and he asked us to make the delivery for him," Penelope said.

"I see," Isaac said. His forehead creased over his blond eyebrows that were so fair they were almost transparent. He sneezed again, and his eyes started watering. "Wait, do one of you have a cat?"

Penelope nodded, then looked down at a few black hairs clinging to her t-shirt. "We do, back at our house. Brogan's cat, actually. Are you visiting her?" Penelope asked. Joey cleared his throat subtly next to her and closed the refrigerator.

"No, I'm...renting the place for a few weeks, until my legal stuff gets sorted out," Isaac said, sneezing again. "I'll be right back. I need to take an antihistamine. I'm really allergic to cats."

"Oh, I'm sorry," Penelope said. Isaac slipped down the hallway and disappeared into one of the bedrooms, returning after a minute. He palmed a pill into his mouth and took a swig of his beer, placing the empty bottle on the countertop.

The air shifted in the room as the front door was opened, the sea breeze rushing past them as they stood around the kitchen counter.

"Good news, love," Brogan's voice called from the entryway, her accent more pronounced than Penelope had ever heard it before. "The old bastard can't completely cut me off...there's a clause in the prenup; he has to pay at least the minimum—" She stopped short when she stepped into the kitchen area and saw the three of them watching her approach.

"What in the world is going on in here? Penelope?" Brogan asked, her face turning red. Penelope thought she looked more beautiful than ever, her wild springy hair shone like silk and her skin radiated healthiness.

"Sorry for the intrusion," Joey said. "We were just bringing your food over."

"Oh," Brogan said. "Where's Jacque?" She tossed a guilty glance at Isaac, then recovered quickly.

"Jacque had an emergency," Penelope said. "His surrogate went into labor early."

"Baby?" Brogan said numbly, placing a hand against her belly. She suddenly looked faint, and Joey went to her side.

"Let me get you some water," he said. Isaac didn't move to help her, just stood staring, unsure what to do.

Penelope handed Brogan the bottle of water she was still holding, and Joey helped her onto one of the kitchen stools.

"I told them I was renting your place," Isaac said.

Brogan looked at him and rolled her eyes. "Then why would they be delivering a week's worth of food to me?"

Isaac looked at her for a few seconds before what she'd said dawned on him. Penelope could almost see the wheels turning behind his eyes. "Oh, right."

"Also, Penelope is our neighbor, she knows what's been going on at the house," Brogan added.

"Are you sure you're feeling okay?" Joey asked. He placed a finger against her wrist and frowned

"I'm fine," Brogan said. "I get these little episodes sometimes. Thankfully, I'm past the worst of the nausea, although I still have a little upsy-daisy here and there."

"So you are pregnant," Penelope said. Brogan nodded weakly. "Congratulations," she and Joey said at almost the same time.

Brogan laughed quietly. "Thank you."

"Calvin must be..." Penelope stopped herself from continuing, remembering that he'd only that morning told her he and Brogan were getting divorced.

"Lucky me," Brogan said. "I gained a child and lost a husband in the same moment."

When he was satisfied Brogan was out of danger of fainting, Joey went back to stand next to Penelope. Isaac sat next to Brogan and took her hand gently in his, brushing the top of it with his finger.

"I'm so sorry," Penelope said. "Maybe he'll come around when he—"

Joey did his throat clearing bit again and nudged her arm gently with his. "We should go and let you two—" he began.

"Guess who got a vasectomy twenty years ago, and never told his current wife about it?" Brogan asked bitterly. "My husband did. The great Calvin Pope." Isaac squeezed her hand briefly then went back to drawing circles on the top of it with his finger. "Here I'm thinking there's something wrong with me, you know, biologically. I went through hell, thinking my body was defective, or that I was being punished for something, or that God had decided I'd already gotten too lucky in life and I didn't deserve a child on top of everything else. My mind went to all of those places. I was convinced of all of them at one point or another. And here he is, allowing me to go through that...knowing full well we would never conceive a child."

"Did you ever ask him to get tested, you know, for fertility?" Penelope asked.

"Sure," Brogan said. "He said he went to his doctor and that there was no problem with him down there. Those were his exact words. I didn't ask him for any proof, stupid me, I believed my husband. And he pointed to his lovely daughter, his proof that he could deliver the goods when called upon. He didn't say it in so many words, but he allowed me think I was the problem."

"Oh, Brogan. I'm so sorry," Penelope said. She looked at Joey, the familiar muscle twitch working in his jaw. It was his anger tell she'd noticed and watched for ever since they first met.

"Yes, I did fall in love with someone who was not my husband," Brogan said with a glance at the man next to her. "I am not perfect either. I had been thinking about leaving Calvin for months. And then, quite unexpectedly..." She touched her stomach again. "I never thought I could get pregnant, so I wasn't particularly careful when...when Isaac and I were together."

"When you came home from your trip last week, you had

just come back from vacation too," Penelope said to Isaac. "Sebastian was teasing you about being with a girlfriend, but I never would've guessed."

"We were discreet," Isaac said. "At least we thought we were. Everything's sort of come apart now."

"When I told Calvin I was pregnant," Brogan said. "I really did think it was his baby." She gave Isaac a sideways glance, but he didn't flinch at the thought of Brogan and Calvin sleeping together, apparently around the same time they had been. "I really did think it had finally happened. I was so excited that I wasn't really thinking about anything else except the baby. Anyway, Calvin went berserk, throwing his wine glass on the floor and threatening to kill me. That's when I learned it couldn't have been his baby, when he drunkenly told me about the vasectomy. Then he accused me of trying to trick him, of attempting to tie him to me financially with a child. He said I was no better than a whore. I just left him there, banging his head against the wall like a madman."

"If I ever see him again, I'm going to break his neck," Isaac said darkly.

"You don't want to do that, man," Joey said. "Or make threats like that in front of a cop."

Isaac spoke through gritted teeth. "He's a monster. I don't care who hears me. I'll kill him."

Brogan put her hand on his chest to calm him. He relented slightly but still radiated anger. "I just came back from a meeting with my lawyer," she said, her voice cracking. "Calvin can prove adultery, obviously, so the prenup is void. But he still should have to pay me the no fault amount we agreed on. It's not much, but it will help until I am able to work again, after the baby is born."

"That's good," Penelope said. "Maybe focusing on the future

is the best thing right now, a fresh start with your baby."

"I'll take care of you," Isaac said. "Both of you." Joey's jaw was still twitching but he remained still.

Brogan's face crumpled and she gave in to the tears she'd been working so hard to hold back.

"Let's go," Joey said under his breath.

"Brogan," Penelope said after they'd gathered up the cooler and were heading toward the door. "Please let me know if I can help you with anything."

She nodded and pressed a tissue to her nose. "Thank you. Oh...there is one thing."

"Sure," Penelope said.

"Take care of Mirabella," Brogan said, tears threatening to spill again. "I can't have her here. Isaac is deathly allergic, and I don't trust Calvin to take good care of her. He's too...he just can't take care of things."

"No problem," Penelope said. "She's happy at our place and we'll keep her for as long as you need." After she turned to go, Penelope stopped. "Brogan," she said.

"Yes?"

"Did you know Sebastian Beauregard was married?" Penelope asked.

Brogan wiped her cheeks and nodded. "It's not something he wanted to be public. But yeah, he and Sara were common law married, I guess you'd call it."

"Do you know her?"

"Only by reputation," Brogan said with a quick shake of her head. "She's from a well-known family in Australia. They're connected, if you know what I mean."

Joey grabbed Penelope's forearm gently and tugged her toward the car.

"Thanks," Penelope said. "Call me if you need anything."

CHAPTER 33

Penelope saw Calvin in a whole new light the next afternoon in the studio kitchen. And Sebastian, too, if she was being honest with herself. She wondered if everyone around her was leading a secret life, one they didn't present to the public, that had nothing to do with their personal realities.

Sara Charles' family was indeed connected, like Brogan said. Joey had called Clarissa when they got home and confirmed her father, while never having been convicted of any crimes, was rumored to be involved in a looming financial scandal, and was associated with organized crime in his country. Joey had strongly urged Penelope to stay away from the woman and her father, and to let the entire matter go.

"I don't want you to get mixed up with people like this, Penny," he said, real worry etched on his face. "Call that detective you met, and tell him what you're thinking. And then that's it."

Penelope had agreed and made the call. Detective Adalbert had humored her and taken the information, then hurried her off the phone after telling her they already knew about the Charles family and were looking into everything.

After the revelations she and Joey had heard at Brogan's condo the day before, the two of them had gone home and collapsed in front of the TV, not saying much, but enjoying a quiet evening together with Mirabella purring quietly on the cushion between them. Penelope felt exhausted from the emotional conversation and the dark moments of her marriage to Calvin she'd shared. All of it had thrown Penelope off balance and was causing her to reevaluate how she felt about him, as well as the last few months she'd spent working for him.

The kitchen she and her team had been working out of for the past few months had been rearranged into twelve workstations, one for each of the potential cheftestants. Each station was outfitted with a propane stovetop and grill grate, thick wooden chopping blocks, metal mixing bowls, a set of cooking utensils, and stainless-steel pots and pans in a variety of sizes.

"Here they come," Calvin said from his seat next to her up on the stage that had been erected in the front of the room. Penelope edged away from him slightly, then caught Joey's eye. He was sitting at one end behind the curtain. He gave her an encouraging nod and she took a deep breath.

The twelve chefs entered the room and found their stations. They were each wearing a matching apron with the *Knives Out* logo stitched on the bib, and had their knife rolls either clutched in their hands or tucked under their arms. Trevor's station was in the third row on the left. He waved at Penelope, and she smiled at him encouragingly.

Trish, the casting director, sat on the other side of Calvin, and Scarlett was to Penelope's left. She'd said a brief hello as she took her seat but had since been scrolling through emails and messages on her phone, stopping only to respond to a few of them.

The writing team was huddled behind Joey backstage in front of a bank of monitors. Camera operators were positioned around the room, zooming in and out shots of the chefs' faces, which the group studied on the monitor intently.

Several production assistants moved throughout the room, checking to make sure all of the contestants were in the correct spots, while sound techs moved from chef to chef to wire them up with microphone packs. One of the techs had clipped a microphone to the neck of Penelope's shirt, and instructed her to feed it down her back and clip it to the waistband of her jeans.

Once everyone was in position and wired for sound, the director stepped out onto the stage in front of the judges' table and called for everyone's attention. He had spiky gray hair, tattoos that covered both of his thick forearms, and looked like he'd be more comfortable sitting in a biker bar than directing a TV show.

"We asked you all here today because you made the cut and passed the first round of auditions," he said in a gravelly voice. "Today is your screen test. Depending on how you do on camera, you will either get picked up for the production, or you will be cut and someone else will take your spot. Understood?"

The chefs responded with murmurs and nods. Penelope could feel the tension rising in the room.

"Now," the director continued, "you will all make your signature dish. These four judges will be watching and tasting your food. No pressure, right?"

A few laughs floated up from the floor.

"You will have a chance to tour the pantry and refrigeration units before you commit to a dish. You are allowed to take notes. No one is to have a device visible at any time. You should've all left your personal devices in the office when you checked in. If we see you consulting a phone or tablet, it's automatic disqualification. Am I clear so far?"

Most of the chefs nodded, while a few just stared straight ahead.

"Now," the director said, "you will have an hour and twenty

minutes to complete your dish, once we start the clock. If you do not finish in time, and these kind folks behind me can't taste your food, you'll be cut."

Trevor tucked his arms behind his back and rocked back and forth on his boots. Penelope knew that meant he was getting anxious. Sometimes when he got too overwhelmed or went too fast, he missed things. Penelope sent him a silent thought of encouragement and willed him to keep calm and complete the challenge.

"And last but not least," the director said, "knives are sharp, boys and girls. Safety first. If you are seen running with a knife, or in any other way acting careless to the point you might hurt yourself or another person on the set, you will be asked to leave immediately."

"Running is okay," Calvin said. "We want to see some energy, just don't stab anyone."

The director let Calvin finish before he spoke again. "All of that being said, we do have a medic on hand for any accidental cuts, burns, falls, grease splashes, grill flareups...you name it. Trust me, boys and girls, I've seen everything and more happen, so please, just be careful. Okay?"

The chefs agreed as a unit, nodding their heads and mumbling they understood.

"All right," he said. "Now you got your ground rules. Okay, you six," he indicated the left row of contestants, "you have five minutes to review the pantry items and to test out any appliances. If you have any questions, find me or another member of the team and ask. Then the rest of you will go."

Penelope watched the chefs file back through the pantry, picking up pieces of produce and pulling proteins from the walk-in. She had to admit she was excited to see what this elite group of chefs would prepare.

"Thanks for letting Joey sit in," Penelope said when Scarlett finally set her phone on the table.

"Sure," Scarlett said. "It's cool he wants to see you at work. He can taste the food too. There will be plenty."

"How many cooking shows have you been a part of?" Penelope asked.

"This is my third," Scarlett said. "The first two didn't make it past the pilot stage. But *Knives Out* has legs. We spent some real money to get the production to where it needs to be. Fingers crossed we finally have a hit."

"How much will they get paid?" Penelope asked. "Unless that's confidential."

Scarlett laughed. "You're on the executive team, so you can see everything. The contestants will get a thousand each per episode, and the grand prize winner will get a payout of fifty."

"So the chef who makes it to the end will get..." Penelope did the math in her head. "Sixty-two thousand dollars."

"For twelve weeks work," Scarlett said. "Plus the title, which you can't put a value on. Winning a culinary competition show raises the profile. They can spin it into more TV appearances, cookbook deals, you name it."

When the first group of chefs got back to their stations, several of them began jotting notes on pieces of paper hidden in a drawer beneath their stations.

"I think number seven is going to take it all," Calvin said, nudging Penelope's arm. He pointed to the pretty dark-haired chef he'd singled out in the meeting the day before. Penelope's stomach did a slow turn when she thought about what Brogan had been through with him, but she managed to smile and say, "I guess we'll see, won't we? I'm curious how she performs under pressure."

Glancing in Joey's direction again, she saw he was watching

at the monitors along with the writing team. He pointed and said something to one of them, and the writer laughed. Penelope loved the way Joey could talk to anyone and was comfortable in any situation.

"Okay," the director said after the chefs were all in position again. "I'm going to call action, and you all rush over to get your ingredients and start cooking. No low blows or actual shoving of other contestants out of the way. Remember the ground rules. Questions?"

When no one raised their hand, he said, "Okay, on my count..." A digital clock suspended from the ceiling behind the judges table lit up as the director counted down from ten. "And go!"

The chefs rushed to the pantry and began grabbing items, stacking their arms with produce, jostling each other for a better position. Trevor was quick to make his selections and was one of the first to get back to his station. Penelope was curious to see what he would make. She thought back to when she'd first hired him, impressed with his sample menu and drawn to his laid-back demeanor. Despite that, Trevor hustled in the kitchen, and always delivered what she'd asked for on time. And she was impressed with his creative input.

Grills were lit and a bowl clattered to the floor somewhere in the back row. A tense silence fell through the room as the chefs worked, the only sounds of knives chopping and oil sizzling in pans. The air turned tangy with the scent of a variety of spices.

"We'll add a dramatic score here, during the dull bits, sound effects," Calvin whispered loudly to her. "Of course, we're not going to show the entire hour and twenty of cooking time either. It will be edited down to fifteen minutes. Just the dramatic pieces will get through to the end."

The half dozen camera operators moved between the tables, pausing to zoom in on a chef's hands at one station, or a boiling pot of water at another. Penelope poured herself another glass of ice water from the pitcher in front of her. Scarlett and Trish mostly kept busy on their phones, but Penelope found she couldn't look away. She kept a close eye on the cheftestants, observing their technical skills and techniques and evaluating their choice of ingredients. Some of them were preparing modern nouvelle cuisine dishes and some were keeping things traditional. None of them looked to be struggling, and she hadn't noticed any flagrant mistakes during the cook time. Penelope couldn't wait to taste all of them.

The director appeared on the stage. "Two minutes left on the clock," he shouted, the digital numbers showing time literally slipping away over their heads. "You should be plating your final dishes now."

"Ten, nine, eight..." he said. "Hands up!"

The dozen chefs held their hands up in the air and stepped back from their stations, then began clapping and congratulating each other.

"Okay, well done," the director said. "You all remembered the rules. Now you'll place your dishes in the warmer at the end of your station until it's your turn to bring up your plates. A production assistant will help you carry them. When you approach the judges' table, be prepared to describe your dish and answer any questions they might have about ingredients or cooking technique. You should have a story about why you chose this particular dish, which shouldn't be difficult, since it's your signature dish, right?

"Okay, number one, you're up."

The rest of the chefs moved their plates into the warmers and the first chef approached the table. He appeared nervous, but when he looked down at the plate he placed in front of Penelope, she saw his confidence take over again. The PA, a young woman Penelope had seen around the studio several times over the past months, placed the remaining two dishes in front of Trish and Calvin.

"Judges, what you have in front of you today is my take on fried chicken and waffles," he said. "I'm from South Carolina and I've been cooking since I was ten years old in my grandma's kitchen. After church on Sundays, we'd go home and make fried chicken for the whole family. She unfortunately passed away last year, so I made this in honor of her memory."

"Great story," Scarlett said, eyeing the plate of food.

"Thank you," he said, then brought his eyes back to Penelope. She'd been introduced as the culinary expert on the panel. They knew her opinion of their food was important.

Penelope took a bite of his dish, and the flavors exploded in her mouth. The chicken was perfectly cooked, the crust seasoned well and expertly fried, the waffle like a sweet pillow beneath it with a subtly sweet syrup with a touch of heat at the end. "This is delicious," Penelope said. "It's a traditional dish but you've elevated it and given us your own take. I think your grandmother would be very proud of the dish you presented today."

The chef in front of her bit his bottom lip and nodded, then brought his palms together under his chin and gave her a slight bow. As he returned to his station, his fellow contestants applauded.

One by one the chefs presented their dishes. Penelope could only point to a couple of missteps from plate to plate, but overall, they were minor glitches in otherwise delightful offerings. From what she could tell so far, they had a very talented group of chefs assembled for the show.

Chef number seven, Ella Banks, approached the table with a plate in each hand, the PA following her with the remaining two. Calvin rubbed his palms together as the assistant set down the dish in front of him, but instead of observing the food, he gazed openly at the attractive young woman.

"Please describe the dish," Scarlett said, poking at a pile of greens beneath a perfectly square piece of seared trout.

"Chefs, um, sorry, judges, you're not all chefs, I know that..." Ella began, the color rising in her cheeks.

"Ella, that's fine, love, carry on," Calvin said, leaning forward. He waved upwards from the plate in front of him to get more scent from the food. "Everything looks completely delicious so you've no need to be nervous."

"Thanks, um, okay," she said.

Scarlett sighed next to Penelope. Ella was just twenty-two years old, and Penelope hoped Calvin didn't have genuine romantic designs on her.

"What I've prepared for you today is a filet of rainbow trout accompanied by a Swiss chard gratin," Ella said a little more confidently.

"And what inspired you to make this for us today?" Calvin asked. He dug his fork in and scooped a large mouthful of the fish and wilted dark greens into his mouth.

Penelope tasted the fish. It was slightly overcooked, but she took into account the time Ella's food had to sit in the warmer waiting to be tasted, and forgave the flaw somewhat. The chard tasted more acidic than she was expecting, and she tried to pick out the underlying ingredients to determine what was giving it that aftertaste.

"I trained in Paris," Ella said, "and this was the first dish Chef taught me in my apprenticeship. I had to master it before Chef would let me to move forward and learn new dishes. I must have prepared it at least a hundred times in that kitchen."

Calvin took another enthusiastic bite. "He taught you well. Bravo."

"Did you taste the greens before plating?" Penelope asked, taking another small bite of them.

"I did, Chef," Ella said unconvincingly, her nervousness returning.

"I'm getting an odd bitterness, an almost metallic taste," Penelope said. "Did you pick up on that too?"

"Yes," Ella said, clearly confused by Penelope's comments. "But I feel I was able to counter that with the gruyere and cream. It tasted balanced to me when the dish was plated."

"Hm," Penelope said, taking a sip of water. "Overall I think this is a nice plate of food, but I'd advise you if something tastes off, for whatever reason, then you have to change the dish so—"

Calvin began to shake violently next to Penelope, then dropped from his chair onto the stage.

"Calvin!" Penelope said, leaping to her feet. "Calvin, what's wrong?"

Trish and Scarlett stood also and looked down at Calvin writhing on the floor. The medic hurried up the center aisle and leapt onto the stage, kneeling down at Calvin's side.

Ella backed away from them while a few of the other chefs moved forward to get a better look at what was happening. Calvin continued to shake uncontrollably on the floor. Joey came out from behind the curtain and stood on the floor in front of the stage, telling the chefs to keep back.

"He's having a seizure," the medic said. Calvin cried out in pain as spittle formed at the corners of his mouth. "We need an ambulance."

Scarlett was on the phone, speaking urgently to someone on the other end. Penelope was on her knees near Calvin's head, watching his body vibrate and feeling helpless.

The shaking seemed to lessen, and Calvin groaned one last time. He became still and exhaled, a big breath of air escaping him, like he was a deflating balloon. His body became still, the painful expression slipping from his bright red face.

An eerie silence fell across the room, like everyone else had stopped breathing at the same time as Calvin.

And then Ella collapsed to the floor in a faint.

CHAPTER 34

"I killed Calvin Pope," Ella kept repeating. She'd gone from being hysterical when she came to, held by Joey, who had gone to her immediately after she hit the floor, to weeping quietly, to her current state—some kind of shock where she kept repeating the same phrase over and over. Ella sat on a stool next to her station, muttering the phrase to herself, a thin blanket wrapped around her shoulders. The other chefs kept their distance from her, although Penelope was pretty sure Ella wouldn't have noticed if they were all taking turns holding her hand. Joey hovered nearby, keeping an eye on her and casually looking at the different items on her station.

Detective Adalbert stood with his fists in his pockets, looking down at the spot where Calvin had died on the stage.

"He's never had a seizure before, you said?" he asked Scarlett.

"I don't believe so," Scarlett said. "He never mentioned anything like that."

Ella's plates were still on the table, the food dying on the plate already.

"He really dug into this dish, huh?" Adalbert said. He bent at the waist and smelled the remaining scraps of food on the plate.

"We're taking all of this in for testing," Detective Zahn said from the floor. "If he was poisoned, we're going to find out."

"I didn't poison him!" Ella shouted from her stool. She retched suddenly, and Joey patted her on the back and mumbled something to her. "Everything I used I got from here," Ella said, behind the hand covering her mouth. "I didn't bring any of my own ingredients into the kitchen, that was the rule!"

"Calm down," Detective Zahn said.

"The chard was off," Penelope said. Detective Adalbert raised his eyebrows at her in a question. She had a sick feeling growing in her stomach, and she thought she might have to rush off and upsy-daisy like Brogan.

"Excuse me?"

The chefs who had gathered near the stage stopped talking among themselves as Trish rushed off. They could hear her getting sick back behind where the writers had gathered.

"We weren't served Swiss chard," Penelope said, hurrying toward the restroom. "That's rhubarb."

CHAPTER 35

"Rhubarb?" Joey asked. He handed Penelope a towel to wipe the sweat from her head after she retook her seat. She'd made it to the locker room behind the kitchen before getting sick, and now her stomach felt empty and relieved.

"Oh my God," Ella said, looking at the leftover leafy greens on her station. "But...it said chard on the bin! I know it did, I saw it when we did the pantry walk through and that's when I decided on my dish."

"It says chard," Detective Adalbert confirmed from the pantry.

"What's the difference between chard and what was it?" Zahn asked, propping her fists on her narrow hips and studying the bin suspiciously.

"Rhubarb," Penelope said. "They look very similar but rhubarb leaves are poisonous."

"But what about rhubarb pie," Adalbert said. "My aunt makes those. Is she trying to kill us?"

"The stalks are fine to eat," Penelope said. "They're bitter so that's why they get mixed with strawberry in pies a lot of the time. The leaves contain oxalic acid, which can be deadly." She looked at Scarlett, who appeared to not be feeling the effects of the tainted dish as much as everyone else. She'd only taken small bites of each offering as they progressed through the tasting, which Penelope assumed was in deference to her trim waistline.

"Why would Calvin have such a different reaction?" Zahn said, appearing unconvinced.

"I know one of the effects of ingesting too much oxalic acid is acute kidney failure," Penelope said. "Calvin just got out of the hospital and maybe his drinking..." she paused, "contributed?"

"The medical examiner will be able to tell what happened," Joey said, rubbing her thigh. "I think you should get checked out too."

"I'm okay," Penelope said.

"Please, for me," Joey said. "I'd like to know that you're okay."

Penelope thought about Calvin writhing on the floor in pain and felt the rolling nausea in her gut. "You're right, let's go."

CHAPTER 36

Penelope sat on the edge of a hospital bed in the Salacia Beach Medical Center, a bag of fluids dripping through the IV attached to her hand. The doctor on duty had ordered a blood screen panel also, but assured her it was only a precaution and that she would most likely be fine in a few hours, once she was fully hydrated and the oxalic acid from the rhubarb leaves had been flushed from her system.

"He said I could go after this one is done and they remove the IV," Penelope said as Joey reentered the room. He'd gone to get her a bottle of water and a bag of chips from the vending machine in the lobby.

"Trish is next door," Joey said. "They have her on her second IV and want to do a few more tests. She's having a lot more nausea than you did. Ella is getting checked out too...she tasted the dish but isn't very ill."

"She didn't taste it enough," Penelope said. When Joey looked at her quizzically, she added, "I mean, I don't want her to be sick, but a chef needs to taste every element on the plate. She obviously rushed through that part or she would have figured out the chard was off."

"Anyway, I'm just glad you're okay," Joey said. "I saw Scarlett too, but she doesn't look sick. Maybe in shock over losing her father, but not physically sick."

"I guess the rhubarb hits everyone differently," Penelope

said. "The doctor said it would take ten pounds or more to kill someone normally, but people with compromised kidneys or other conditions..."

"Acute kidney failure. That's what Scarlett was talking about with the doctor when I walked by," Joey said. "Not a nice way to go."

A nurse stepped in behind Joey and checked the fluid bag suspended next to Penelope on a metal pole. Satisfied it was finished, she gently removed the tape holding the needle in place on her hand. Once she was done, she handed discharge instructions to Joey, and helped Penelope stand up from the bed.

Stepping into the hallway, Penelope almost ran into Scarlett, who was hurrying along the corridor, her eyes full of tears, with Bernice following close behind.

"Scarlett," Penelope called out, but she didn't stop. Scarlett pushed through the front door just as Bernice grabbed her by the arm. Scarlett shook her off and pushed her way outside, Bernice following close behind.

CHAPTER 37

Penelope got to the studio early the next morning and went directly to the kitchen.

No one had been in to clean since the audition. There was food strewn across the individual stations and plates had been overturned onto the floor. The police had taken samples from Ella's plates, and the ones up on the stage, and then pronounced the area clear for the studio staff to enter. Penelope supposed since she had been working out of the kitchen for the last few months that it fell to her to deal with the mess, although she didn't really have to. Thinking about how upset Scarlett had seemed at the hospital the previous afternoon, she decided to deal with it, as a small way of helping her out.

She wasn't the only one at work that day. Penelope had passed two of the *Knives Out* writers in the hallway. One of them gave her a quick glance then looked away as they continued on, neither of them saying a word to her.

Penelope sighed, pulled out her phone, and sent Javier a text.

Got a job for you. A messy one. Pays well.

The bubbles appeared in the messenger app and then the reply: *10-4.*

She typed a response and pocketed her phone, then headed for the pantry area. The bins were full of wilting produce, except the one marked *Swiss Chard* that had been cleared out by the police evidence team. They'd also taken samples from a few of the other bins, and left a few of the refrigerator doors hanging open. The earthy smell in the kitchen was on the verge of being unpleasant, and caused a slight stir in her stomach. Penelope was pretty sure she wouldn't be eating rhubarb again for a very long time.

Penelope unlocked the door to the office in the back of the kitchen and took a seat behind the desk. Normally she kept the door open when she worked in there, but the rotting smell of food was more than she could take with her still tender stomach.

Logging on to Pope Productions internal system, Penelope found herself in a new portal she hadn't had access to when she was a department head on *Severed Lives*. She had executive level access now because of her role on *Knives Out*. Opening the project site for their show, Penelope began clicking different links to open reports and review files.

She opened a folder labeled *Contestants*, and twelve links appeared, one for each of the chefs that were trying out for the show. Clicking on Trevor's first, she found his professional headshot, his CV, a criminal background check, and psychiatric evaluation. She clicked on a link that led her to a personal essay Trevor had written, talking about why he wanted to be cast for *Knives Out*, and a six-page questionnaire about his culinary likes and dislikes, inspirations, and the dishes he expected to prepare on camera. She scrolled through his answers, which all seemed to reflect what she knew about him.

The final link led her to a recap document that listed personal information, including proposed salary, residency and tax information, and a line labeled "insured amount." Penelope did a double take when she saw the dollar amount next to it, which she knew was more than Trevor made in a year.

Rubbing her finger on her chin, Penelope navigated away

from the personnel file and clicked on the production folder, clicking through several links before she found the document she was looking for. Opening the audition produce order she scanned down through the items, tapping her knuckles lightly on the desk. Her eyes stopped when they arrived at *Swiss Chard: one carton.* There was no rhubarb anywhere on the form.

Penelope sat back in her chair and stared at the screen, the words blurring and coming back into focus. She tapped her phone next to her on the desk and pressed Francis's number.

"Hey Boss," Francis said over the buzz of wheels on the road. "I hope you didn't leave anything in the truck because I just passed Salt Lake City. It's too late to turn around now." Penelope had called Francis and told him to pack it up and head home the day before. Even though he had a long drive ahead of him, Penelope caught herself wishing she could be there, heading out of there with him.

"Ha, good one. How's the drive been so far?" Penelope asked.

"Good," Francis said. "It's a beautiful part of the country out here. How are things going there?"

Penelope looked at her computer screen again and shook her head. "Don't ask. But I'm okay. Hey, I had a question for you."

"Shoot," Francis said.

"What's the name of the delivery guy you were friendly with?" Penelope asked. "You know, from the produce supplier?"

"Oh, my man Mike," Francis said. "Why, he mess something up?"

"Maybe," Penelope said.

"That doesn't sound like Mike, but you know, everyone makes mistakes," Francis said.

"That's true. Okay, I'll give him a call," Penelope said. She slid open the top drawer and felt inside, feeling around for the envelope of Sebastian's letters she'd left there a few days earlier. "You're taking lots of breaks, right? You know you can stop anywhere along the way and expense it all back to me." Feeling nothing inside, she pulled the drawer out all the way. The envelope was gone.

"I know not to push it," Francis said. "I'm being safe. I got to admit though, I'm ready to be back home."

"I know what you mean," Penelope said, staring at the pens and paper clips organized neatly in the drawer, then sliding it closed. "Check in with me later so I know you're okay."

"Will do," Francis said and hung up.

Penelope stood up from the desk and thought for a minute. She knew she hadn't taken that envelope out of there herself. So who had been going through her things?

A thought occurred to her and she sat back down, opening the personnel files again and clicking on the folder for Ella Banks.

CHAPTER 38

"Hi Trish," Penelope said, knocking lightly on the doorframe to the hospital room. Penelope had walked the four blocks from the studio to the medical center for a quick follow up with the doctor. Her fluid levels were good and her blood work showed no sign of lingering toxins. While she was there, she decided to look in on Trish, who they had kept at the hospital for further evaluation.

Trish was gathering up her things and stuffing them in an overnight bag, her discharge instructions and a prescription bottle of pills lying on the hospital bed.

"Hey," Trish said. "You just caught me. I'm out of here thank God."

"I'm glad to see you're feeling better," Penelope said.

Trish nodded and picked up the vial of pills. She read the label and shook her head, then stuffed it in the front zipper of her bag. "I'm okay, they're just worried about my blood pressure. It gets triggered when anything else happens medically. I have to take this medicine for a while until they can reevaluate me."

"I'm sorry to hear that," Penelope said.

"Me too," Trish said. "Not exactly the news I was hoping for, but what are you going to do? How about you? I thought you were okay since they released you yesterday."

"I am okay, just got the all clear on my labs," Penelope said.

"Lucky you."

"Trish, do you mind if I ask you something?"

Trish looked at her suspiciously. "That depends. What do you want to ask me?"

"It's about Ella Banks," Penelope began.

"Who?" Trish asked.

"The pretty young chef who—"

"Poisoned me, and killed Calvin? Yeah, I remember her. What do you want to know?"

"How did she make it onto the audition pile?"

Trish zipped up her bag roughly and slung it over her shoulder. "What do you mean? She made it there like everyone else."

"But I couldn't help notice Ella's credentials were...less remarkable compared to the other contenders. She's a lot younger too."

"She met the minimum requirements and passed the background and psych evals. She was a legit cast." Trish moved toward the door.

"So, there was nothing odd about her making it into the audition meeting?" Penelope asked. She had the sense that Trish wasn't saying something important.

"No," Trish said, becoming agitated.

"Okay," Penelope said. "I'm sorry if I upset you."

Trish was breathing a little heavy as she passed, hefting her bag out through the door. Penelope watched her go, wondering what she was holding back. Trish paused halfway to the exit and turned, lumbering back to where Penelope waited.

"Are you investigating what happened? You and your cop boyfriend?" Trish asked.

"No," Penelope said. "I just want to know why the food we ate was tainted and how it got that way. I have an idea, but I'm looking for some confirmation."

Trish adjusted the bag on her shoulder and the vial of pills inside her bag rattled. "You didn't hear it from me," she said under her breath, "but I was told to add the girl to the finalist pile and to present her alongside the others at the meeting. I didn't do anything wrong. I'm asked by clients lots of times to push people to the top of the pile, and I won't do it if they aren't qualified for the job. But this girl was, and I did it as a favor to Pope Productions."

"Okay," Penelope said. Trish had a sheen of sweat on her upper lip and she looked like she needed to sit down. Penelope was worried she'd spiked Trish's blood pressure with her questions. "That's helpful, thanks."

"I don't want to get any calls from the cops," Trish said. "I'm not looking for any trouble. Like I said, I did nothing illegal or even unethical. I didn't falsify any reports. I was told if I could help Pope out with this request, that I could count on more projects coming my way. I figured it was no skin off my nose and if I get a few more calls...what's the harm?"

"Don't worry, I won't say anything," Penelope said. "Like you said, there's nothing to it anyway. You didn't break any laws."

Trish nodded warily and turned back around to leave.

"One last thing," Penelope said, calling after her. "When did Scarlett ask you to push Ella to the top of the pile?"

Trish looked back at her and shook her head. "You got that part wrong. It wasn't Scarlett who made the request."

Penelope took a few steps closer to her. "Who then? Was it Calvin? I could see how much he liked the looks of her just in the few minutes they spent together."

Trish laughed. "Yeah, we could all see that. No, it wasn't Calvin. Bernice Mabley is the one who called me. You know, the girl in the office who runs everything over there at Pope."

Penelope thought for a few seconds. "Scarlett must have told her to call you," Penelope said. "Bernice is the administrator, so she would've handled a request like that on behalf of Calvin or Scarlett."

Trish shook her head. "No, she specifically told me to put the candidate forward and to keep it to myself. Something about the selection process not being tainted for the Popes beforehand."

"But why do you think Bernice would ask you to put Ella on the top of the stack?" Penelope asked.

"Maybe she and Ella are family," Trish said with a shrug. "That's usually the reason people get a leg up in this business. They know somebody, or they owe somebody a favor."

CHAPTER 39

"Family," Penelope mumbled as she stared at the computer screen back in her office at the studio.

She opened the folder on Ella Banks again and pulled up her personal information. Ella was from San Francisco, had attended a culinary program there right out of high school, and then spent a few years in France before coming back to work at a restaurant in her hometown. All of that matched up with the background Trish had provided, and aside from the DUI there was nothing negative on her record at all.

Penelope clicked back to the main personnel folder and saw the executives for the show listed there, including Scarlett, Calvin, the director, and herself. Bernice was listed as Executive Assistant to the team and Penelope opened her link, leaning forward to look at the different entries listed under her name. She didn't find anything there that she didn't already know about Bernice, meaning not much at all.

Finding the folder for *Severed Lives*, she opened it, hoping that maybe there would be more information there. Finding no additional clues about Bernice, she was about to exit out of the folder when she noticed Sebastian's file. Opening it up she scanned through his entry, her mouth dropping open when she saw the amount listed in the INSURED column. Pope Productions had taken out a policy on Sebastian for over three million dollars. Clicking around to see how that compared with the other actors on the movie, it was definitely the biggest amount out of all of them.

Penelope picked up the phone on her desk and called the produce delivery company. "Hi, this is Penelope from Pope Productions," she said to the dispatcher, who grunted something sounding like "okay" in response.

"Can you have Mike, our regular delivery driver, call me when he gets in?" she asked.

"Why, there something wrong with your order? You have to call the salesman with any complaints. My guys just drop the stuff off, they don't deal with any paperwork."

"No, it's...I just want to ask him about something," Penelope said.

"Okay," the dispatcher said grumpily. "He's on the road till probably four. Give me your number."

Hearing footsteps and unfamiliar voices on the other side of her office door, Penelope stood up and peered outside. Javier was in the kitchen with two guys she'd never seen before.

"Look at this mess," Javier said with a shake of his head.

"Thanks for coming," Penelope said. "I've approved hazard pay for you to deal with it."

Javier laughed and introduced Penelope to his friends, one of whom had already started clearing off one of the stations. "We'll get it scrubbed down and back into shape, no problem."

"Great. I'll be in here a few more minutes finishing up some things if you need me." She stepped back into the office and went back to the file on her screen.

There wasn't any personal information listed for Bernice Mabley that she could find. Penelope sighed and sat back in her chair, thinking. After a few minutes she got up and headed down the hall to the front office.

Bernice was at her desk, her head ducked down as she

worked on her laptop.

Penelope knocked and she looked up quickly, then back down again after waving her inside.

"Sorry to interrupt," Penelope said, "but I wanted you to know I have a crew in the kitchen cleaning up the mess from yesterday."

"Good," Bernice said. The door to Scarlett's office was closed behind her and Penelope had seen the lights were off in there when she passed by in the hallway.

"Have you heard from Scarlett today?" Penelope asked. "I'm just wondering how she's doing."

Bernice looked up at her again and closed her laptop. Her eyes were red and slightly puffy as if she'd recently been crying. Her hair was perfectly coifed as usual, but she'd come to work in jeans and an untucked button-down men's style shirt instead of one of her well-tailored outfits.

"She's dealing with everything that's happened fine, but of course it's not easy on her. There are arrangements to be made, legal things to take care of."

"It's good she has you for support at work," Penelope said.

Bernice smiled ruefully. "Thanks. Scarlett is strong, and she thinks she can get through everything on her own."

"I think you're right about that," Penelope said. "And you probably would know better than anyone. How long have you worked for the Popes?"

"Eight years," Bernice said, then cleared her throat.

"What were you doing before that?"

Bernice sighed. "I was working as a PA on a movie in LA when I met Scarlett," her voice broke slightly. "I'd never heard of Salacia Beach before. Or Pope Productions."

"What was Scarlett doing in LA when you met? Was she working on the movie too?" Penelope asked.

"No, she was scouting stuntmen for Calvin for some movie of his that never got made," Bernice said, her eyes shining with tears. "She was there to meet my brother Paul and a few other guys he worked with."

"I'm sorry," Penelope said. "I didn't mean to bring up anything upsetting."

"I'm not upset," Bernice said sharply and wiped her cheeks with her palms. "I tagged along when my brother came to meet with Calvin, interviewed for this position, and never left. Scarlett has things under control. Everything will be better soon, once we get through..." she trailed off.

Penelope felt like she'd probably asked enough questions already. She turned to go, then stopped at the door. Bernice had opened her laptop and had begun typing again. "Hey, did you happen to know Ella Banks before she auditioned?"

"No," Bernice said quickly. "Wait, who is Ella Banks?"

"She's the chef who—"

Bernice showed Penelope her palm. "Of course. No, I don't know any of the contestants. Production is on hold until further notice."

CHAPTER 40

"Bernice Mabley, from the office," Penelope said to Joey when she got home.

"Who?" he asked. He was wearing his bathing suit and had just been about to go for a swim in the pool when she got home. Mirabella ate daintily from her bowl on the kitchen floor, pausing every few bites to look up at her and Joey talking.

"She's the one I thought I saw at the restaurant that night, remember?"

"The one who disappeared and you weren't sure if it was her?"

"Yes," Penelope said. "I'm pretty sure it was her."

"So this Bernice greases the way for a chef to get the opportunity to audition for a reality show and...tricks her into poisoning Calvin?" Joey asked.

Penelope bit her bottom lip, hearing the skepticism in his voice. "I'm not sure. But there's got to be a reason she wanted Ella to be at the audition. And I feel like Sebastian's and Calvin's deaths can't just be a coincidence."

"I see where you're going, but I'm not seeing where all of the pieces fit," Joey said. He pushed a bowl of salsa he'd made toward her and handed her a blue tortilla chip. Penelope took a bite. "On one hand you have a philandering playboy actor, who has a wife no one knew about, from a let's say, influential family. On the other hand you have..."

"A terrible husband with a wandering wife," Penelope said. "Who was also a liar about big things in his life."

"They don't go together, from what I can tell," Joey said.

"Wow, this is good," Penelope said, distracting herself from the frustrating puzzle she was trying to unravel.

"Thanks," Joey said. "Your chef chops are rubbing off on me."

Penelope crunched on another chip then said, "I looked at Ella's audition forms and she listed the dish she made for us as the one she'd most likely prepare on the show."

"What reason could Ella have to poison Calvin?" Joey said.

"I can't think of any. The poor thing was a mess afterwards. She doesn't strike me as a criminal mastermind either," Penelope said. "And I couldn't find any connection between her and the Popes, no work history, nothing. She's been out of the country most of the past few years."

"Except, Bernice made sure she was in the room for some reason," Joey asked.

Penelope's phone rang and she picked it up. "Hello? Oh, hi Mike, thanks for calling me back."

Joey sipped his beer and watched her expression as she spoke. When she hung up, she set her lips in a line.

"What's up?" Joey asked.

"That was our regular produce delivery guy," Penelope said. "He said he was slipped a hundred bucks cash at the loading dock to swap the rhubarb in for the chard the morning of the audition."

"By who?" Joey asked.

"Bernice," Penelope said. "Well, he didn't say her name, but he described her perfectly." Joey blew out a low whistle.

"She told him it was part of a prank, to fool the contestants," Penelope said.

"Well," Joey said, "there's nothing illegal about swapping one leafy green in for another."

Penelope deflated a bit. "I know. But she was obviously trying to get us to eat it...she got the rhubarb in the pantry, where it was mislabeled, and made sure a contestant who would cook it was in the room."

"Okay," Joey said. "What is her motive? Is she a disgruntled employee?"

"She always seems happy at work," Penelope said. She sighed and ate another chip.

The sound of a car approaching drifted through the front windows and Penelope went into the hallway to see who it was. Scarlett stepped out of a dark blue sedan and headed toward Calvin's house, an empty garment bag slung over her arm, while her driver waited in the car, a phone pressed to his ear.

"Scarlett's here," Penelope said. "I'm going to go over and see if she needs any help."

Joey sighed. "I know I can't stop you. Do you want me to come too?"

Penelope looked down at his swim trunks and Mirabella who was looping her way around his ankles. She could tell they were both looking forward to their time by the pool. "No, I'll just be a minute."

CHAPTER 41

Scarlett opened the front door of her father's house and smiled when she saw Penelope standing there.

"I don't want to intrude," Penelope said. "I just wanted to see if I could help with anything."

Scarlett put a hand on her shoulder and squeezed. "Thank you. I just came to get one of Calvin's suits for the funeral."

Penelope followed her through the hallway and into the kitchen. The entire inside of the house had been cleaned, every surface polished, every cushion straightened, and every window wiped clean. The slight tang of disinfectant lingered in the air. The white boards on the floor where the wine had spilled and sat for days showed no sign of staining.

"When is the funeral?" Penelope asked.

Scarlett studied two suits on hangers she had brought down from upstairs. "Three days from now, Thursday at two at Vincent's Funeral Home. I hope you can be there."

"Of course," Penelope said. "How are you holding up?"

"Okay," Scarlett said, rubbing her finger on one of the suit's lapels. "Calvin wasn't one for dressing up. I hope one of these still fits him."

"I didn't find the shoes you were talking about but what do you think about these?" a man called down from the top of the glass staircase.

"Which ones are they?" Scarlett called up to him. "I can't see."

"The brown ones," the man said, coming down a few steps to show her.

"You can't wear brown shoes with a gray suit," Scarlett said.

"Who's going to see his feet?" the man asked, he stopped short when he saw Penelope standing in the kitchen.

"Paul, this is Penelope from next door," Scarlett said. He lifted up the shoes in a wave.

"Paul," Penelope said. "Are you Bernice's brother?"

"I am," he said. "Have we met before?"

Penelope took a few steps closer the staircase. "I don't think so. But I've heard her talk about you."

"Paul came to help with things," Scarlett said. "For the funeral."

"Anyway, I can't find the black shoes," Paul said. He trotted the rest of the way down the spiral stairs to show her the shoes he had found.

"I guess brown will be okay," Scarlett said. "I mean, who cares what he's wearing at this point?"

Paul held the shoes against the suit jacket and shrugged at Scarlett, his back to Penelope. He lifted the pant leg up and held it over his arm, brushing the fabric with the palm of his hand. A strange feeling of déjà vu came over her when she looked at the back of his neck and the shape of his shoulder. Her eyes fell to his fingers and saw the blackened nail on his third finger. A metallic taste bloomed in the back of her throat.

"What do you think, Penelope?" Scarlett asked. "Do you think the shoes matter?"

Penelope's tongue felt thick in her mouth. She shook her head and stared at Paul, the image of him placing the gun into Isaac's hand racing through her mind.

"Are you okay?" Paul asked, his forehead creasing in concern.

"Yeah, I..." Penelope said, looking quickly at Scarlett, who also appeared concerned. "Sorry, I haven't been feeling completely myself since...you know...what happened."

"Penelope was at the audition too," Scarlett said to Paul. Penelope saw a flash of something registering with him, but his expression remained the same.

"I think the shoes are fine," Penelope said, recovering. "They were his, and he must have liked them enough for them to be in his closet," she added lamely.

Paul studied her for a second longer then set the shoes down on the table. "Did you want to get anything else while we're here?"

"No," Scarlett said. "I think that's it."

"Penelope, I'll be in touch with you about the show," Scarlett said as she walked her to the door. Paul had stayed in the kitchen to zipper the suit and shoes into the garment bags after a hasty goodbye to Penelope.

"Do you think you'll continue on with it?" Penelope asked.

"We've spent a lot of money on it," Scarlett said. "Calvin would've wanted us to press on."

"Okay, whatever you need," Penelope said. She waved from her front porch as they pulled out of the driveway and sped away, then went inside her house and called Detective Adalbert.

CHAPTER 42

The next morning at the studio, coffee in hand, Penelope surveyed the freshly cleaned kitchen space, and silently thanked Javier for his hard work. She'd come in to inspect the kitchen and clear out the pantry and submit the payroll hours for Javier and his friends. She was going to request they receive a nice bonus on top of the per diem rate the studio typically paid for pickup work. They'd definitely earned it.

To her delight, Javier had also cleared out the pantry, storing away what could still be refrigerated and used, and tossing everything that had spoiled. A detailed loss report was on her desk, which she would attach to the budget forms she had been asked to file for her piece of the production. Javier had just saved her a couple of hours of inventory time.

Sitting down at her desk, she turned on her computer and waited for it to warm up and sipped her coffee. The office door was open and a flash of movement out in the kitchen caught her eye.

"I'm in here," Penelope called out, then logged into the computer. A beeping noise sounded and the words ACCESS DENIED flashed on the screen. She typed in her password again with the same result.

"You've been cancelled," Bernice said from the doorway.

"What?" Penelope asked with a laugh. "Cancelled?"

Bernice was dressed like her old self again in a bright blue dress that fit her small frame like a glove and shiny black stilettos. She leaned on the doorway with an amused look on her face, one hand tucked behind her thin waist. "You're out. You can leave."

"Excuse me?" Penelope said, standing up.

Bernice's hand appeared from behind her back. She was holding a small silver pistol, which was just as stylish looking as Bernice was. "Get out!" she shouted, which caused Penelope to jump. She moved around the desk carefully, keeping her eyes on the gun.

"What are you doing, Bernice?" Penelope asked.

"You're the one who called the police," Bernice said. "You had my brother arrested." Bernice backed into the kitchen, keeping the gun pointed at Penelope's chest.

"I...he's the one who gave Isaac the gun," Penelope said. "He killed Sebastian."

"No," Bernice said, frustrated. "Isaac killed Sebastian. Don't be stupid. You saw it for yourself."

"Isaac didn't know the gun was loaded," Penelope said, stepping out into the kitchen. She glanced at the door behind Bernice, which suddenly seemed very far away. She definitely wouldn't be able to outrun a bullet if she tried to make a break for it. She decided to inch toward it slowly and keep Bernice talking.

"Kind of like Ella didn't know she was cooking with rhubarb," Penelope said.

"Calvin was a sick old man," Bernice said. "He died of natural causes. If he hadn't wrecked his kidneys with all of his drinking, he'd be fine."

"Sebastian was killed for the insurance money, wasn't he?" Penelope asked. "You file the policies with the insurance company. You found a way to route the payment to yourself and then you'd just fix the books to make it look like it had been paid."

Bernice faltered for a second, then her expression hardened. "I didn't do anything for myself."

"You set everything in motion," Penelope said. "You positioned all of the pieces and then let them play out. You altered the call sheet for *Severed Lives* that day, swapping Paul for the regular prop handler. You had the chard replaced with rhubarb, and you made sure Ella was chosen to audition for the show."

"I did," Bernice said with a shrug. "Nothing wrong with any of that. Legally speaking."

"This right here feels pretty illegal," Penelope said.

"What, this?" Bernice said, straightening her arm and tilting the gun back and forth. The overhead lights glinted off of the metal. "I'm just showing you my gun. My brother's gun, actually. He thought you'd want to see it."

"Let me guess," Penelope said, the final piece clicking together. "Paul stole this one from Heston Berkley too. Just like the one you both used to kill Sebastian. That was the movie Paul was working on when you met Scarlett in LA all those years ago. The dates match up."

"I didn't kill anyone!" Bernice shouted. "Don't be so stupid! What gives you the right to poke around, hiding things in your desk. You don't really work here. You'll be gone just like all of the other ones." She raised the gun and aimed, and Penelope dropped to her knees, shielding her head with her arms. "Get up!" she shouted.

Penelope stood back up on shaky legs, leaning on the nearest kitchen station. "You're the one who took Sebastian's envelope from my desk?"

"Of course," Bernice said. "His girlfriend mailed it to the

studio, along with the first picture they ever took together, ripped in half. He was thinking of quitting the project, heading home to patch things up with her. Like an idiot."

"And you had to have him killed while he was still working on your set," Penelope said.

"Get out," Bernice said, waving her gun toward the door.

"Where are we going?" Penelope asked.

"You're going to take a drive," Bernice said. "You've been stealing from Pope Productions. I have all of the evidence of your embezzlement, which I'll be turning over to the authorities. I'm going to let them know that I confronted you with what I found, and you were distraught when you left. Driving off a cliff is the perfect way to end your embarrassment. You knew you'd never work in this business again with something like that following you around."

Penelope stopped, her shoes squeaking against the floor. "I won't go. You'll have to shoot me right here."

"Don't tempt me," Scarlett said.

"Shoot me," Penelope said.

"Shut up!" Bernice screamed. She raised her arm again and her finger tensed at the trigger. Penelope closed her eyes and raised her hands in front of her face, an ineffective shield against a bullet.

Her eyes flew open when she heard a loud crash. Bernice was on the floor, a cascade of metal bowls and pans clattering on the floor around her. Javier had her in a bear hug from behind, and the two of them struggled against each other on the floor. The gun skittered toward Penelope and she kicked it away. It came to a rest against the back wall, next to the door leading to the locker rooms, where she assumed Javier had come from.

"Get off!" Bernice spat, scratching at Javier's thick forearms.

Penelope stumbled to her office and fell across her desk, pawing the top of it until she found her phone. She dialed 911 with shaking hands.

"What are you doing here this morning?" Penelope asked after she hung up with the operator.

"I came in to say goodbye," Javier said. "And to thank you for the work."

CHAPTER 43

Penelope walked along the edge of the cove at Monastery Beach, heading for the lone figure sitting on the damp sand near the water. The sky was overcast and the sea choppy. Scarlett had on a thick gray hoodie that hid most of her face. Pieces of her black hair whipped her face as she stared out at the ocean.

"Thanks for coming," Scarlett said as Penelope sat down next to her on the sand.

"Why did you want me to come here?"

"I wanted to show you where it all started," Scarlett said. "I've lost them both now, Mom right out there," she pointed at the choppy water, "and Calvin...Dad...well, I lost him that day too. Life was never the same for either of us."

"Scarlett, I'm so sorry about everything that's happened," Penelope said.

"He didn't even try to save her," Scarlett said. "She disappeared under that last wave while I watched."

Penelope kept quiet, following Scarlett's gaze out to the horizon.

Scarlett dropped her forehead onto her arms and then sat up straight, pulling her phone from the front pocket of her sweatshirt. "Now I'm really alone. My parents and now Bernice. They're all gone." She showed Penelope a picture on her phone of her and Bernice on the beach, embracing and smiling at the camera. Penelope remembered the one on Bernice's desk and it looked to have been taken the same day.

"We've been together for eight years," Scarlett said, shaking her head.

"I know she was a valuable part of the company," Penelope said. "I can't imagine—"

Scarlett laughed and shook her head. "No, we've been together for eight years. And now she's been arrested on conspiracy to commit murder along with Paul."

"Oh, I'm so sorry," Penelope said. "I didn't know."

Scarlett shrugged and wiped a tear from her cheek. "We were discreet."

"Detective Adalbert called," Penelope said. "Bernice was—"

"She thought she was helping," Scarlett said, then laughed bitterly. "She thought it was time for Calvin to retire. He kept acting like he was on his way out, but kept hanging on. His health was declining..."

"So Bernice thought she'd hurry him along," Penelope said.

"Yeah," Scarlett said. "It's my fault for complaining so much about him. I told her he would sell me the company for three million dollars, so she took out a policy for that exact amount and had Sebastian killed for the payout. Who would do something like that?"

"None of this is your fault," Penelope said. "You're a survivor, and you're strong." She reached over and rubbed Scarlett lightly on her back. Scarlett began to weep and leaned into Penelope. She put her arms around Scarlett's shoulders and hugged her while they watched the waves ripple onto the sand together.

CHAPTER 44

The funeral home was crowded with mourners for Calvin's viewing, and the procession to the cemetery was made up of over three dozen cars following the hearse through town. Joey and Penelope stood near the gravesite after the ceremony was over, watching the mourners pay their respects to Scarlett and Brogan, who sat next to each other during both the service and the burial.

When Jacque and his husband, who was holding their new baby in a tight bundle, got to the front of the line, Brogan stood up and held their newborn son a minute, a brief moment of happiness in the otherwise somber day.

When the crowd had finally dispersed, Penelope made her way over to the women.

"I know it's difficult to hear, but that was a beautiful service," Penelope said. Isaac had been hovering behind Brogan throughout the funeral, keeping an eye on her even when he was speaking to friends who stopped to shake his hand.

"Thank you," Brogan said. "I think we're going to be okay."

Scarlett nodded. "We are. We still have each other."

Penelope hugged them both.

CHAPTER 45

A few days later, Penelope and Joey were at the airport, waiting for their flight back to New Jersey.

"Are you happy to be heading home?" Joey asked.

"I don't think I've ever been happier to be on my way home," Penelope said. "Although I did love that little beach house. Brogan is going to sell it along with the mansion. Too many ugly memories there for her, she says."

"I suppose things worked out for Brogan, timing wise," Joey said.

"Yeah," Penelope said. "She and Calvin were still legally married so there wasn't time for him to change his will before he died." Penelope thought about the years of anguish Brogan had gone through during her marriage and thought things had probably worked out for the best. "Brogan got his assets, and Scarlett got the business."

Scarlett had called a meeting the Monday after the funeral and announced that Pope Productions was going through some internal restructuring, and that production on *Knives Out* would be postponed for at least a month or two until they could get their company staff realigned.

"If you'd like, we can bring you back out to consult on the show," Scarlett said. "But I realize you'll probably have another project going before long."

"Keep me posted," Penelope said. "But I do think I'd like to stick to the east coast for a little while."

"Understood," Scarlett said. She handed Penelope an envelope. Inside was a thank you card, and two first class plane tickets home.

"What's this?" Penelope asked, pulling out a third, smaller travel ticket.

"That's for Mirabella," Scarlett said. "If you want to take her home."

Penelope had hired Javier on full time to Red Carpet Catering, creating a new position for him as team leader for West Coast productions. He had been so excited at her offer he crushed her into a hug, which was out of character for the normally reserved man she'd gotten to know over the past few months. Trevor had picked up work on another catering crew and was still going out on auditions. She was sure she'd see him on TV before too much longer.

Penelope and Joey got settled in the first-class cabin, Mirabella's carrier in between them on the seat. A flight attendant appeared next to them with two glasses of champagne, which they accepted gratefully.

"I think Mirabella will make a great Jersey Girl," Joey said, tapping his glass to Penelope's. "Although we might have to shorten her name. You know, Bell, or Mira maybe. Mirabella is a mouthful."

Penelope laughed. "Maybe. We'll see how she likes the colder weather."

"As long as she's with us, she'll be taken care of," Joey said. He sat up suddenly and patted the front pocket of his shirt. "Oh no," he said in alarm.

"What's the matter?" Penelope asked.

"I forgot something," Joey said, fumbling in his pockets.

Penelope sat up, looking around on the floor. She set her champagne glass down and said, "What did you lose, Joey?"

"Maybe it's in here," Joey said. He set his glass down too and opened Mirabella's carrier. Pulling her out gently he said, "Whew. Here it is."

"What are you talking about?" Penelope asked, looking at the cat. Her deep green eyes blinked up at her and she meowed. She picked Mirabella up and saw something shiny dangling from her collar. "Oh, Joey."

Penelope's eyes blurred over with tears and she blinked them away. A diamond engagement ring glittered in Mirabella's long black fur.

"Penelope Sutherland," Joey said. "Will you marry me?"

"Yes!" Penelope said breathlessly.

They kissed, and Mirabella curled in between them on the seat.

Joey eased off her collar and freed the ring from it, sliding it onto Penelope's finger.

"I love you," Joey said. "I can't wait to spend the rest of my life with you. Wherever we are, when I'm with you, I'm home."

"I love you too."

SHAWN REILLY SIMMONS

Shawn Reilly Simmons was born in Indiana, grew up in Florida, and began her professional career in New York City as a sales executive after graduating from the University of Maryland with a BA in English. Since then Shawn has worked as a bookstore manager, fiction editor, convention organizer, wine consultant and caterer. She has been on the Board of Directors of Malice Domestic since 2003 and is a founding member of The Dames of Detection. Cooking behind the scenes on movie sets perfectly combined two of her great loves, movies and food, and provides the inspiration for her series.

The Red Carpet Catering Mystery Series
by Shawn Reilly Simmons

Henery Press Mystery Books

And finally, before you go...
Here are a few other mysteries
you might enjoy:

THE SEMESTER OF OUR DISCONTENT

Cynthia Kuhn

A Lila Maclean Academic Mystery (#1)

English professor Lila Maclean is thrilled about her new job at prestigious Stonedale University, until she finds one of her colleagues dead. She soon learns that everyone, from the chancellor to the detective working the case, believes Lila—or someone she is protecting—may be responsible for the horrific event, so she assigns herself the task of identifying the killer.

Putting her scholarly skills to the test, Lila gathers evidence, but her search is complicated by an unexpected nemesis, a suspicious investigator, and an ominous secret society. Rather than earning an "A" for effort, she receives a threat featuring the mysterious emblem and must act quickly to avoid failing her assignment...and becoming the next victim.

Available at booksellers nationwide and online

Visit www.henerypress.com for details

THE HOUSE ON HALLOWED GROUND

Nancy Cole Silverman

A Misty Dawn Mystery (#1)

When Misty Dawn, a former Hollywood Psychic to the Stars, moves into an old craftsman house, she encounters the former owner, the recently deceased Hollywood set designer, Wilson Thorne. Wilson is unaware of his circumstances, and when Misty explains the particulars of his limbo state, and how he might help himself if he helps her, he's not at all happy. That is until young actress Zoey Chamberlain comes to Misty's door for help.

Zoey has recently purchased The Pink Mansion and thinks it's haunted. But when Misty searches the house, it's not a ghost she finds, but a dead body. The police suspect Zoey, but Zoey fears the death may have been a result of the ghost...and a family curse. Together Misty and Wilson must untangle the secrets of The Pink Mansion or submit to the powers of the family curse.

Available at booksellers nationwide and online

Visit www.henerypress.com for details

MURDER AT THE PALACE

Margaret Dumas

A Movie Palace Mystery (#1)

Welcome to the Palace movie theater! Now Showing: Philandering husbands, ghostly sidekicks, and a murder or two.

When Nora Paige's movie-star husband leaves her for his latest co-star, she flees Hollywood to take refuge in San Francisco at the Palace, a historic movie theater that shows the classic films she loves. There she finds a band of misfit film buffs who care about movies (almost) as much as she does.

She also finds some shady financial dealings and the body of a murdered stranger. Oh, and then there's Trixie, the lively ghost of a 1930's usherette who appears only to Nora and has a lot to catch up on. With the help of her new ghostly friend, can Nora catch the killer before there's another murder at the Palace?

Available at booksellers nationwide and online

Visit www.henerypress.com for details

STAGING IS MURDER

Grace Topping

A Laura Bishop Mystery (#1)

Laura Bishop just nabbed her first decorating commission—staging a 19th-century mansion that hasn't been updated for decades. But when a body falls from a laundry chute and lands at Laura's feet, replacing flowered wallpaper becomes the least of her duties.

To clear her assistant of the murder and save her fledgling business, Laura's determined to find the killer. Turns out it's not as easy as renovating a manor home, especially with two handsome men complicating her mission: the police detective on the case and the real estate agent trying to save the manse from foreclosure.

Worse still, the meddling of a horoscope-guided friend, a determined grandmother, and the local funeral director could get them all killed before Laura props the first pillow.

Available at booksellers nationwide and online

Visit www.henerypress.com for details

CPSIA information can be obtained
at www.ICGtesting.com
Printed in the USA
LVHW081559030919
629785LV00011B/122/P